THINGS THAT GO "BAA!"

IN THE NIGHT

Roger Pond

Things that go "Baa!" in the Night

Tales From a Country Kid

ROGER POND

Pine Forest Publishing

First Printing, June 1992

Second Printing, October 1992

Library of Congress Catalog Card # 92-80125

Publishers Cataloging-in-Publication Data

Pond, Roger, 1944-
Things that go "Baa!" in the Night
1. Humor
I. Title

ISBN #0-9617766-2-5

Published by Pine Forest Publishing
314 Pine Forest Road
P.O. Box 289
Goldendale, WA 98620

Cover Design by Edna Rix

Printed in the United States of America

To all who have provided ideas
and encouraged my writing,
with scant regard for their own safety.

Contents

From Ghoulies and Ghosties
And long legitty Beasties,
And Things that go bump in the night,
Good Lord deliver us.

Old Cornish Prayer

ACKNOWLEDGMENTS

All of these stories have appeared in newspapers throughout the U.S. and Canada that use The Back Forty news column . I am especially grateful to those publishers who have found it in their hearts and budgets to subscribe to The Back Forty these many years.

Thanks also to Bonnie Beeks for many hours spent reading and correcting the little glitches in my writings; and to Mike Combelic for uncanny speed and accuracy in electronic page layout.

A special thanks to my wife, Connie, for help all along the way; and her almost childlike belief that there has to be some money in this business, somewhere.

Buffy's Wild Ride

One of the drawbacks of part-time farming is the high cost of equipment that you only use once a year. The part-timer or hobby farmer just can't afford the tractors and trucks a guy really needs to do things right.

Consequently the hobby farmer is constantly making do with what he has or can borrow from the neighbors. Even though a person may own two cars and an Oriental pickup, the animals are always too big or too dirty to transport in what you have available.

That's what happened to my cousin, Dean, when it was time to take Buffy the bull home after breeding season. Dean has a small farm with some pasture and it just seemed natural to have a few cows around. Then, if you are going to have some cows it's just natural to keep a bull for a few weeks, so you'll have some calves.

I should stop here and explain that Buffy is not something you would normally name a bull. You can name your sheep, pigs, dogs, or daughters Buffy, but this is not good for a bull.

A bull needs a name like Mark Domino 707, Hillsdale Blackmar John, or simply Red — but never Buffy! With a name like that it's a wonder the old bull wasn't totally sterile.

But Buffy had to go home, and Dean agreed to take him. So he borrowed a horse trailer and went to work getting the car rigged-up with a trailer hitch.

Of course a person wouldn't normally haul a bull in a horse trailer, either, but this was OK for Buffy. He was just a big pet anyway, and would probably ride in the car if the door was big enough.

With just a little coaxing the bull walked into the trailer like a kid's pet horse, and they were off. So here's Cousin Dean heading down the road with old Buffy in the trailer when he hears a sudden thump and starts to put on the brakes.

But before he could turn around to look back, here comes Buffy in the passing lane. The trailer hitch had come loose and the bull was wheeling it down the highway at 50 miles an hour! And being an Angus, Buffy had no horns to blow.

There was one little window in the front of the horse trailer, and all Dean could see was a big brown eye as Buffy went by. Then the trailer left the road and took out two flamingos and a cast iron lawndog before impaling its tongue in a lovely antique Desoto.

My cousin says the folks who owned the lawn ornaments and the old car were really nice about the whole thing, and the insurance agents got the forms filled out once they stopped laughing. The bright spot is that Buffy wasn't hurt — at least not physically.

Old Buffy still sires good calves, according to the bull's owner, but every time a horse trailer goes by on the road it lengthens the calving season by two weeks.

What Now Coach?

There's nothing like a good basketball game to create some excitement in a rural community. When the team is winning, everyone is a master of roundball strategy. And when we're losing it's only a matter of days before the same people who have been asking how many fouls a player is allowed will begin calling out defenses from the stands.

I try to keep quiet at the high school games. The only person I give any advice is my son; and he knows I'm full of bologna and doesn't let my suggestions bother him.

The game has changed so much, I'm not sure I understand it anymore. When I was a kid we didn't have all these terms like "power forward" and "point guard." In those days power forward was the first gear on the team bus, and a point guard was a short guy who never made more than one foul shot.

Every time I hear someone giving the players advice from the stands I think back to my first game in the sixth grade. Even though all of us kids had been shooting baskets since we could stand up, we weren't well-versed in the game.

The coach grabbed five kids off the bench and made two of them guards, two forwards, and one a center. That's the only way you played in those days: Two guards, two forwards, and a center.

Our center was a big kid named Jim, who had moved in from Arizona the year before. Jim's family moved a lot and he lost a grade or two in the process — that's one of the reasons he was so big.

He couldn't shoot much and couldn't dribble a lick, but Jim could rebound, so in he went. We had one play: The forwards and center went after the defensive rebound, tipped it to the guard waiting at the foul line, and the guard took off down the floor while a forward and the other guard ran down the sidelines.

If we didn't get a shot on the fast-break we might as well give the ball to the other team and let them shoot it again, because that was "our play". But our play usually worked, and in this first game we were up by eight points at halftime. Then, the coach put in the second string. Eight points pretty well puts the game out of reach for sixth graders.

So we all came out, and I'm sitting there on the bench beside Jim when he says, "Well, I got a 'C.'" (And you could tell he was kind of proud of it.)

"What do you mean you got a 'C'?" I asked.

"They gave me a 'C' for dribbling and shooting and stuff," he said.

Stanley was sitting on the other side and said, "They don't grade you in basketball, you dummy. What ever gave you the idea you got a 'C'?"

"You go up there and look at the book on the table," Jim shot back. "They've got a 'C' beside my name!"

"That's because you're the center, you dope," Stanley said. "They'd better not be grades, 'cause I got an F and Roger got a G!"

14

Shooting Rats

Solid waste disposal has become a prime concern and a thriving business in many parts of the country. Thirty years ago who would have thought burying garbage would become a major industry? Now the business is taken over by big companies with names like Environmental Dumps or Eco-Trash.

Regardless of a person's views on solid waste, we've come a long way from the time when shooting rats at the dump was our main Saturday night entertainment. When I hear kids today say they're bored and have nothing to do, I always regret the closing of the dumps. This generation will never see the rats we used to have.

A dump wasn't a big thing in those days — just an acre or two where people could come and throw out anything they didn't want. Or folks could come and trade — you'd throw out some old cans you didn't need and pick up a set of handlebars for your bike or an old handbag for your sister. Where I grew up every community had a dump, and most townships did, too. It was sort of like a bowling alley: If your community didn't have one, you felt second-class.

Nobody had a bulldozer to cover the trash in those days, and I really can't tell you for sure whatever happened to it. After the dumps were closed everything was covered with dirt, but in the meantime the rats did their best to tidy up the place.

I wasn't old enough to drive to the dump and had to tag along with my brother when we went rat shooting. Somebody had to hold the light, and my brother said I was too young to handle a gun.

As far as I can remember there really wasn't much shooting on those trashland safaris. Most of our time was spent jumping at noises. Anyone who hasn't heard about a rat running up a kid's pant leg, has never been to a rat shoot. That story was told at least once each hour, and before long everyone had eyes like Barney Fife and couldn't hit a fifty gallon drum, let alone a speeding rat. Then an old bedspring would twang and we'd be four feet in the air grabbing our pant legs.

When they closed the dumps and replaced them with "sanitary landfills," that pretty well ruined the rat shooting for future generations. I don't know where a guy could go for that kind of sport these days.

Some folks look at landfills as a blight on society — an object of scorn and disgust. Most of us would like to have them somewhere far away.

But if I had a few thousand acres with a big canyon or two, I don't think I'd mind leasing-out some land for a landfill. It's better than a prison, in my opinion.

There are two things I would want in my lease though: 1. All trash will be compacted severely and buried immediately. 2. If any part of this agreement is broken, the landowner gets first shot at the rats.

What Now Brown Cow?

A recent visit to a modern dairy barn reminded me of how far we have progressed in milk production. Management and efficiency are the key words these days, and most dairymen even hire someone else to do the milking.

When I was a kid nobody hired people to milk cows. That was like hiring someone to wash your dishes — the ultimate self-indulgence.

Besides, a person couldn't milk someone else's cows in those days. You had to know the cows on a first name basis or they would kick the snot out of you. Even if you were lucky enough to survive what the cows could dish-out, the equipment would finish you off.

Our milking was done in stanchions where a guy had to sidle up next to a cow and convince her he was pretty much harmless before he could even think about putting the milker on her. In those days we used the old Surge milkers that hung from a strap over the cow's back.

The person doing the milking had to squeeze in between two

cows and hang the belt over the one to be milked, while trying to convince the cow behind him she would be hamburger if she so much as lifted a leg. Then he would hang the milker on the belt, attach the cups to the udder, and adjust the belt for that particular cow.

It worked remarkably well for most cows, but there were always exceptions. The exception I remember best was an old, brown cow named Susie.

Susie had a trace of Ayrshire blood in her, giving her those big, brown eyes with an inordinate amount of white showing around the edges. Susie always looked frightened, and she had good reason: We threatened to kill her nearly every day.

When we opened the milking-barn door, Susie would jump through it like a lion bounding through a hoop, and then she would slide about halfway down the concrete alley behind the stanchions. By the time she calmed down and got into a stanchion that cow was panic stricken. It was like she had never been milked before.

You would think an animal that had entered the barn twice-a-day for four years could find a stanchion without getting lost, but Susie never perfected it. She would run to the other end of the aisle and whirl around before the other cows got halfway into the barn. Then she would jam her head between the stanchion and the frame holding it, and remain stuck until someone belted her in the nose to back her out.

This was one of those cows we had to use the kickers on. For those who haven't seen kickers, they were made of two pieces of steel, shaped to fit around a cow's hocks. The two leg attachments were held together by a chain, which could be adjusted to hold the cow's hocks together so she couldn't lift a foot to kick you.

These contraptions worked fine until a cow figured out how to kick with both feet, and then you had a bovine jackass on your hands.

When I enter a modern dairy I'm always amazed that a dairyman works all his life for a nice milking parlor and some civilized equipment, and then he hires someone else to do the milking. Somehow it just doesn't seem quite fair.

Improving Your Lie

The increasing popularity of golf is bringing new problems to this ancient sport. Once a game for the rich and well-heeled, golf has become a sport of the masses.

The game's newfound popularity is frustrating for those who thought they were doing something other people couldn't afford. It's like fox hunting: There's little pleasure in shouting "Tallyho," when everyone else is yelling, "There goes the varmint!"

Golfers have the same problem. A guy can practice his game until the cows come home, but if he doesn't know the jargon, he'll always feel out of place. A more experienced golfer may not beat you on the scorecard, but he'll always thump you with his terminology.

My brother, for example, is an expert golfer. Merlin tells people he plays 18 holes in the low 70's. He golfs in the 60's on really good days, but if it gets much colder than that he just stays home.

As a public service to younger golfers, I have decided to clarify some of the terms heard on the golf course. These should help one understand the more serious guys who wear those funny, little hats.

Here are a few of the most important terms:

1. Improving Your Lie: The habit of creating a story and then telling it over and over until folks start to believe it. See "Winter Rules."

2. Winter Rules: A loosely defined custom that permits a golfer to improve his lie in either the fairway or the rough. Otherwise he is only allowed to tell it in the clubhouse.

3. Addressing the ball: A time-consuming chore, seldom needed unless you hit the ball a long way and think someone might mail it back.

4. Provisional ball: Any golf ball your son has not taken from your bag. It's yours, provided he doesn't want it.

5. Handicap: The hat golfers wear when they can't find the one they want.

6. Caddy: Car driven by older golfers.

7. Subaru: The vehicle I park next to the Caddies.

8. Mulligan: A free shot often allowed when playing for fun. Usually awarded after a bad shot on the first tee, second tee, or somewhere else on the course. Also a type of stew popular with golfers.

9. Pitching Wedge: A frequent response to a bad shot.

10. Chip-in: A frequent response to several bad shots. Chipping in generally involves quarters and dimes.

11. Putting Green: Chipping-in with larger amounts.

12. Tee: A little stick the golfer sets a ball on.

13. Teetotaler: A golfer who counts the number of tee's found that day. Normally the most trusted member of a group.

14. Awlshett: An old Scottish word, used like "Tallyho" to warn other golfers the ball has been struck.

I hope this clears things up to some extent. Readers may also want my new home video, "How To Play Golf Good Without Hardly Trying."

Potluck

"What time does it start? When will it be over? How much does it cost?" I asked.

"All I know is it's going to be February 21, and it's a potluck," the boy replied.

"A potluck?" my wife shouted. "They can't do that to me! What am I going to fix for a potluck?"

I tried to calm her by reading from the dictionary. "It's right here — Potluck: 1. the regular meal available to a guest for whom no special preparations have been made. 2. whatever is offered or available in given circumstances or at a given time."

"See it's no big thing," I told her. You just go and put some things on the table and whatever's there people have to eat."

Ha! My wife knows better than that. You try that at the Methodist Fellowship Hall or the Centerville Grange and you will be laughed right out of the county.

Anyone who thinks a potluck is something you just find on the table has been sheltered from the real world of eating. The potluck is a feast of tradition, thinly disguised as "a little something I threw together this afternoon."

While it may have begun as a simple sharing of food between families, the potluck quickly escalated into knock-down-drag-out culinary competition.

The potluck was perfected in the era when young women prepared for such dinners the way a diver trains for the Olympics. The days when new dishes were practiced like a triple back-flip from the high board. People became famous at potlucks.

You remember them as well as I do: Aunt Lucille's Baked Beans, Aunt Juanita's Dinner Rolls, Mrs. Steiner's Deviled Eggs. Dishes no else dared to make, because they knew better. Trying to duplicate someone else's dish would be the height of folly.

You can still find them out in the countryside, at the Cattleman's Field Day and the Grange meetings. Women who can start with a bag of red beans and wind up with chili. People who arrive with the biggest bowl of food you ever saw and go home with nothing: The ultimate compliment.

As more women enter the 9 to 5 work force, many fear the era of the oldtime potluck is coming to a close. There just isn't time to prepare food the way folks used to.

Today's woman may view potlucks with a certain amount of hostility. The casual comment of "Oh, let's just make it a potluck," is becoming the modern equivalent of, "Why don't we just step outside and settle this thing once and for all?"

Sometimes the only way to cope with an unexpected potluck is to look at the humorous side. That's what my wife did as she rummaged through the refrigerator, collecting ingredients for her basket of dinner rolls.

"What's so funny?" I asked.

"My yeast has a use-date of April 1987," she replied.

An Uphill Battle

"Why did you have to shoot a deer on the steepest ridge you could find, so now we have to spend all day dragging it out? How did you get over here anyway?" the boy asked.

"Well, I saw a deer headed this way and it looked like a buck; so I just sort of followed along until I came upon this one. Besides this will be easy once we get him out on the ridge here," I said.

I knew my son, Russell, was perturbed that my deer was much larger than the one he shot a couple of weeks earlier; and griping about the long drag was just his way of expressing displeasure. A father should be considerate of a boy's ego.

"This would be easy if it weren't such a big deer. Maybe I should just stick to those with dinky, little antlers like some people shoot," I suggested.

I could see that the boy was getting tired and my efforts to cheer him up weren't succeeding. Sometimes you just sense these things, and other times you can tell by the rocks rolling down the hill at you.

Some fathers would be upset at a youngster questioning their wisdom, but Russell and I have this unspoken agreement. We know that some days I could be wrong, and some days he could be wrong; but on the average it won't matter by the time we get the deer to the truck.

My mind went back to all those times the boy has miscalculated my judgment and those rare instances when I was actually in error. There was the time we fished for hours without catching a thing and Russell was convinced there were no fish within 20 miles of that river.

"Just be patient. We have several hours until dark," I counselled. And sure enough, just before dark we went home totally skunked.

Then, there was the time he said, "You should have shot that forkhorn. Now you only have one day to hunt, and you'll wind up without any deer at all."

But on the last day of the season, I saw this deer trot over the hill toward the other side of the ridge, so I followed it. Before long I walked around a point and there was a nice big buck with a decent set of antlers, and I got him.

When I showed Russell where the deer was, he looked up the ridge and said, "I'll just go on up and drag him out for you."

After hiking up the hill and seeing the deer, the boy asked, "Why did you have to go and shoot a deer on the steepest ridge you could find, and then we have to spend all day dragging it out?"

"Maybe I should just stick to those small ones with dinky, little antlers that won't catch in the brush when we drag 'em," I countered. "And stop rolling those rocks down the hill!"

I guess this is typical of my philosophy about raising kids: Sometimes you have to admit they're right, and the rest of the time you had better just stay uphill.

Fat Man — In Good Condition

"Pot-bellied Pigs. Excellent Conformation. Males $600, Females $1200." That's what the ad says.

"How could that be?" I thought. Pot-bellied pigs — excellent conformation? That's like saying "Fat Man — In Good Condition."

What is excellent conformation for a pot-bellied pig? I know what makes a good razorback, but pot-bellies are another matter.

With a razorback you should be able to pick the hog up by the ears — and if he balances, that's good conformation. For pot-bellies, one might paint stripes on them to see if they roll straight, or maybe the best ones would float in a bathtub.

The new-found popularity of pot-bellied pigs for pets has me baffled. We had pigs like that when I was a kid. We called them "tail-enders."

In every bunch of pigs there would be a few that just didn't grow right. After all of their siblings had gone to market, we'd still have the tail-enders that were too small to sell, but too big to roast.

Those pigs were like college kids: All you could do was keep feeding them in the hope that someday they would grow up and make something of themselves.

Our tail-enders had pot-bellies, too. You could spot these pigs clear across the lot — just by looking for the ones with inflated centers. How were we to know these pigs would be valuable as pets?

It's like everything else in my life: I was ahead of my time. If we had those pigs today, they'd be worth a fortune.

A fellow could run an ad saying, "Tail-enders. Excellent conformation. Barrows, sows, gilts, and boars. $600 if you feed 'em. $1200 we feed 'em."

I'd have to admit those tail-enders were excellent companions. They were always friendly, and a guy could keep them around forever. Those pigs were just like part of the family.

On the other hand, I don't think I'll ever get used to the trend toward making livestock into house pets. I can understand miniature donkeys and pygmy goats and things like that, but there's something about keeping a pig in the house that makes me nervous.

Surely folks will write and say pigs are one of our cleanest animals, smarter than dogs, and friendlier than kids; but I've cleaned the hog barn often enough to be skeptical.

I can understand how a person might become attached to a little pig with a pot-belly and big, floppy ears. Still, the idea of sitting down to a plate of ham and eggs while old Porky snuffles around under the table is just another way to ruin breakfast as far as I'm concerned.

Beware Of Animals

A recent visit with college seniors in animal science reminded me of the importance of childhood experiences in shaping students' values and ultimately their careers. Of four college seniors I talked with, all had pets when they were youngsters and all went to college to become veterinarians.

Of course four years of college can do a lot to a person and not everyone can get into vet school even if they still wanted to; but it's interesting that childhood experiences with animals can have such an effect upon a person's career.

The power that animals have over people was first illustrated to me when I was a freshman in high school. It was Friday morning and an assembly was scheduled for 9:00 a.m.

You will remember a high school assembly could be anything in those days. One of our best was the guy who dressed like Buffalo Bill and threw knives at his wife; and you have probably seen the man with the trained snakes and the rollerskating goat.

At my school, assemblies like these were subtly blended with programs where ministers spoke on the evils of throwing

27

knives, and criminals demonstrated their talent for picking locks.

Then, every so often we would have a music program where a woman from the Big Plain Symphony Orchestra would demonstrate the many notes one can make with a flute.

Attendance was not required for school assemblies. But if you didn't go, you had to sit quietly in the classroom thinking up reasons why you needed to go to the library.

So we tried to dope-out the assembly. If we saw the Buffalo Bill guy drive up, it was a sure thing the assembly would be exciting. If a lady drove up in a white van, we knew it was full of instruments and a long morning of flute music was in store.

This particular morning nobody had seen anything, when the announcement came over the P.A. system, "There will be an assembly at 9:00 a.m., and we need four volunteers who are not afraid of animals."

Suddenly everyone's ears perked-up. A line comprised of everyone who wanted to help with the assembly was quickly formed outside the principal's office. Change began to jangle from faded Levis, as each student fished around for the dime that was normally required to attend an assembly.

Nine o'clock came and the gym was full. Students waited expectantly for the program to begin. Then, the stage curtain slowly parted and there was the honorable Howard Swartz, former student from the Julliard School of Music, seated in front of a piano!

We knew we had been had: The four volunteers were needed to move the piano.

When we called him on it the principal replied, "I didn't say there were any animals. I just asked for volunteers who aren't afraid of them."

Horses For Homeless

Each time I see a segment on TV about the homeless, I try to come up with ideas that would help these people; and sometimes the more I think, the more confused I become.

Just this week I read about some homeless folks protesting to demand better housing — and against city ordinances which forbid panhandling and camping downtown. It's hard to get used to a homeless person protesting his housing, but I guess we can learn.

Then I read about the homeless person who went to court to prove panhandling was a right of free speech and protected by the First Amendment. It seems you can settle almost anything with a protest or a lawsuit these days.

But when I see one of these demonstrations I always think of old Frank Johns (not his real name), who lived near my hometown. I often think Frank would have been homeless if he had lived in the city.

But he didn't. He lived in the country and about once a week we would see him riding his horse back home from town.

Everyone knew that Frank could have driven his old Ford to town, but without his horse he never would have gotten home.

His horse was like a designated driver, and a lot more dependable. The horse never touched a drop of alcohol in his life, and could find the barn in the worst of storms.

Once the horse found the barn, it was up to Frank to find the house. I guess that's one of the things that separates horses from people, a horse can always find his way home.

When Frank spent an exceptionally hard day in town, you would see him riding along about dark, with the reins in his lap and both hands on the saddle horn, confident the horse would make all the right turns. Once in a while the boys at the tavern would loosen Frank's cinch a little, causing some pretty fancy trick-riding near the edge of town.

I think of the old fellow each time I see the homeless on television and the shelters they are expected to live in. It's not hard to understand why many would rather camp along the river than go to sleep in one of those shelters.

But why are they so set on living in the middle of the city? That still has me baffled. And then I begin to wonder if the cities would be better off to buy each of the homeless folks a horse, so they could find their way back home the way Frank did.

You can see all of these solutions become more complicated when a person thinks about them for awhile. My idea of providing horses could backfire on the person who sold the horse.

How would you like to unload old Ringbone, only to see him come walking home with a guy on his back and a grocery cart dragging behind?

And how would you like to be walking down the street when some guy walks up and says, "Hey buddy, can you spare a flake of hay?"

Chicks Under Pressure

Nearly anyone who grew up on a farm can remember the arrival of baby chickens. This happened in March at our place and there was a lot of preparation before the little peeps arrived from the hatchery.

The brooder house was cleaned and disinfected, a bale of peat was scattered for bedding, and the brooder lights were all checked. Everything had to be just right for the health and safety of the chicks.

When the boxes full of chicks arrived, the little fuzz balls were taken carefully from the box and placed under the brooder. This was the most dangerous part of the operation, especially if Mother had helpers.

A recent cartoon in Bob Artley's "Memories of a Former Kid" captures the scene exactly. Mother is removing chicks from the box and instructing the older children on how to handle them carefully. At the same time the two-year-old is reaching into another box and lifting a chick by its head.

The baby of the family was always the most interested in

baby chicks, as well as the most dangerous. Mothers learned quickly that you don't give a chick to a two year old without taking some precautions.

There is little danger that the youngster will drop a chick. Quite the contrary, the little ones are so fond of baby chicks squeeze them like toothpaste in a tube. You have to watch them closely and keep a close check on the youngster's grip.

I can remember handing my little brother, Merlin, a baby chick when he was only about two years old. You should have seen his eyes light up! The chicks eyes got pretty big, too, but we got it away from him just in time.

Excitement is contagious, and everyone was surely excited by the time the kids got all of those chicks out of the box. That's one of the problems with kids: They always want to help with things they aren't quite ready for. Then, when they're big enough to help, they are no longer interested.

The days when every farm had a flock of chickens are long gone. People just don't have time for that kind of thing anymore.

It's too bad, I think. Feeding the chickens gave the kids something to do and a chance to develop a little responsibility. Of course some kids were more responsible than others, but we all had a chance at least.

My wife and I took a tour in Europe several years ago, and noticed that farms in countries like Switzerland always had a few chickens running around. Out tour guide said chickens that are allowed to run loose are called "happy chickens" in that country, and bring a higher price at the grocery. It seems the more exercise they get the more they're worth.

I wish we had known that when I was a kid. Some of our chickens would have been worth a fortune in that kind of market.

Stalking The Trophy Tree

She thought we were lost. How ridiculous! I've never been lost in the woods, hunting a Christmas tree.

My wife fails to recognize my natural sense of direction — the uncanny ability to navigate over hills and hollows until I don't have the slightest idea where I am. She admits I can tell up from down, but gives little credence to my east or west.

"No, we aren't lost. The sun goes down in the west and we walked down the logging road to the east, then we turned north. That means the main road is just on the other side of this swamp here," I assured her. "If you follow my tracks you can stay out of the water."

My wife was dubious about why we needed to hike through the woods to hunt Christmas trees. We get our tree from the national forest, where a person buys a $5 tag and searches millions of acres for a wild and elusive evergreen.

There's something about buying a tag and having an entire forest to hunt in that awakens my Daniel Boone complex. The forest is beautiful in the winter, and I see no reason to whack

33

down the first tree we see and retreat to civilization.

My kids look forward to our annual Christmas tree hunt like the dog anticipates his bath. "When do you want to get the tree?" I ask them.

"Anytime is fine," they say, "As long as we don't have to go."

My wife went, though, and we wanted a tree for the church as well as one for the family. I had barely closed the car door when Connie said, "Here's one that's just the right size for the church."

But the family tree is my responsibility, and I wasn't just looking for a dinky, little tree or some scraggly, old fir bush. I wanted a trophy tree. A big, fat one that could stand up to the four-dozen lights and three-pound ornaments we get on sale each year after Christmas.

We hiked down a logging road and out into a swampy area, then took a shortcut through the woods, and before I knew it we were way the heck out in the middle of nowhere — and still no tree.

Then my innate sense of direction (and a passing pickup truck) told me there was a road nearby. And right near the road, though slightly hidden from view, was the best-looking tree we had seen all day. It's amazing how nice they look when you find them close to the car.

Some readers might wince at the thought of going out in the forest to cut a live tree, but there is really nothing to be concerned about. The forest we visit has billions of trees, many of which are just slapping each other on the branches and fighting for a little sunlight. When a person cuts one of these trees, its neighbors drip sap with gratitude.

Christmas tree hunting is one of the privileges of living in an area bounded by national forests. A federal token for our depressed economy the rest of the year.

But what if everyone went out to the national forest and cut a tree for Christmas, one might ask. I don't think we have to worry about that. If anyone else wants to go, my kids can talk them out of it.

Phonics Needs Phunding

School funding has long been a problem for rural communities. Nearly every day a person can read about schools eliminating sports or shutting down the school buses for lack of funds.

Taxes are always a disagreeable subject; but I don't think I will ever vote against a school levy. That's because I will never forget the days of my youth and the school I attended.

It was a good school in general, and we had some good teachers. But I think kids get a better education today — and better facilities are partly responsible for this.

I grew up in the days when schools were made of brick and plaster. The floors were wooden and sounded as if they were hollow, creating sounds that carried from one end of the building to the other. Insulation was almost unheard of.

To top it off, each kid had a big pair of clodhoppers or cowboy boots to clomp around in. Class changes sounded like The Wave at a professional football game.

I don't know how schools are constructed in The Netherlands, but I can tell you that a kid with wooden shoes would have closed down St. Paris Elementary.

The walls in our school were pretty thin, too. If a kid was really bright and had good hearing, he could complete three grades at once without leaving his seat.

Reading was taught by phonics in those days, and my third grade teacher was an expert at this. She was a little bit deaf, and could shout "A - E - I - O - U" in such a way that two janitors learned to read by the sounds coming from the third grade room.

The first thing we learned when I was a kid was the ABC's. Some of the smarter kids picked-up the whole alphabet; but a lot of us just got the ABC's.

At the same time the first-graders were learning the ABC's, Mrs. Lambert (not her real name) was giving the third-graders their A - E - I- O - U's. If you were standing in the hall (or the cloak room), you listened to "A, I, O, U, X, Y, Z" until you couldn't remember which grade you were in.

Mrs. Lambert had it in for us farm kids and was fond of saying, "You kids that live on a farm won't ever have to worry about jobs or money. When you need some food, all you have to do is go out and kill a pig."

I can remember standing in the hall and listening to the second grade reading, "Run, Spot, run,"; when suddenly from the third grade Mrs. Lambert would interject, "Go kill a pig!"

Each time I go to the polling booth to vote on a school levy or a bond issue, I think about my old school.

Some folks vote "yes" on the levy because they want a better band room, or a stage, or more computers.

I'm in favor of those things, too. But most of all, I just like to see nice, quiet rooms with good insulation.

How To Tickle A Pig

The animal welfare controversy has led to some unusual research at agricultural universities. Even though humane treatment of animals is an essential part of commercial livestock production, scientists are finding it hard to prove whether the animals are really happy or just going along with the program.

Researchers have taken the bull by the horns so to speak and are making some interesting discoveries. Dr. John McGlone at Texas Tech University has found, for example, that pigs which are handled in a friendly manner do better than those which are treated roughly.

The scientist says pigs which are patted regularly will grow faster than those not patted. His studies show that pigs especially enjoy having their ears tickled, and slaughter hogs will do better if someone tickles their ears on a regular basis.

I have no problem with this: If people can talk to their plants, I suppose a guy can tickle his pigs if he wants to. On the other hand, I have concerns about encouraging folks to become friendly with their slaughter animals.

That's what happened to the famous Montana artist, Charlie Russell, and his trapper friend, Jake, when they acquired a pig one spring. I can't find the book where the story appeared, and Charlie told it a lot better than I can, but it seems he and Jake were holed up on the south bank of the North Fork and doing their best to keep fresh meat on the table.

Then, just when the two trappers were getting mighty tired of venison, Jake found a small pig with its head caught in a syrup can. Old Jake said, "Hot dog! This little oinker is going to be fresh pork before fall, and he'll be mighty fine eating." (Or words to that effect.) So he and Charlie took the pig back to the cabin to feed for a few months.

The pig was a friendly little guy and by the time fall rolled around was just like one of the family. But as the nights got a little colder Jake started talking about all the nice ham and bacon the pig would make. He always had an excuse, however: The pig wasn't big enough, Jake's knife wasn't sharp, or the weather was too warm.

This went on until one afternoon when Charlie and Jake arrived at the cabin to find the pig had gotten in and scattered food from one end to the other. The little rooter was covered with flour and had wallowed in everything he couldn't eat.

That did it! The next morning Jake was sharpening his knife, when he handed Charlie the rifle and said, "That pig's big enough, go out and shoot him and stick him."

Charlie said, "Not me. He's your pig! You shoot him."

Jake began fussing and fuming like a spoiled child. Then he took his rifle and tromped up the hill behind the cabin.

After Jake had been gone a few minutes, Charlie went out to feed the pig. As he stood there watching the animal eat, a shot rang out and the pig fell over dead.

Jake came trudging down the hill, his rifle still smoking. He pulled out his knife and said to Charlie, "You don't reckon he knew who did it, do you kid?"

Early Retirement

I read recently that an increasing percentage of Americans are taking early retirement, to the point that industries are worried about a shortage of experienced workers. It seems once the old guys quit, nobody knows for sure where they put the Phillips screwdrivers (or the milk of magnesia for that matter).

What's worse, the younger workers don't seem to care about screwdrivers, and many wouldn't know a Phillips from a monkey wrench. That's the scary part.

This rush toward early retirement is just the opposite of what was happening during the late '60s and '70s. In those days we kept pleading with the old-timers to retire so some younger person could finally make some advancement.

But they wouldn't quit. These folks had grown up during the depression and the idea of giving up a job is something that generation just never got used to. Some of them started their job during a depression and then kept at it until everyone else felt the same way.

Those were the years when mandatory retirement became

popular. I was teaching high school in western Ohio during the late '60s when there was no mandatory retirement in that state. At the same time teachers in Indiana were forced to retire at 70.

Some of our best teachers in western Ohio were those who had retired from Indiana schools. We had others, of course, who could barely find their way back across the border each evening. They should have taken their retirement and enjoyed it.

But now people are quitting early and employers are asking the psychologists, "Why do these people want to retire so soon?"

I don't know what the psychologists are saying, but I think people in my generation will admit we are getting lazy. Whereas the previous generation wanted to work forever, we have a group coming on who would love to retire at 40.

When psychologists were advising, "Take it easy, learn to relax so you will be prepared for retirement," my generation was saying, "Ha! Just give me a decent retirement income, and I'll relax 'til my body melts down."

This is the "have it all" generation. The group that says, "Oh yes, I'm taking early retirement this year, but Lucille still has a few years to go."

This may work for some men, but let's not forget the 50-year old woman who called her husband one afternoon and said, "You won't believe this, but I just won $4 million dollars in the lottery! Pack your clothes!"

"Wow!" says the husband, "Where are we going? What should I pack? Winter clothes or summer clothes?"

"Both," she says. "I want you out of the house by 6:00!"

Shear Madness

I guess I've put this off long enough. It's nearly summer and I still haven't completed the wool harvest.

Experienced readers will notice I say "wool harvest," rather than "sheep shearing." It's the same thing, of course, but this newer terminology doesn't scare the sheep so badly.

I'll do nearly anything to avoid scaring the animals. I figure the sheep have enough adrenalin as it is, and there's no point in spooking them up.

Besides, the word "harvest" has such a nice ring to it. It conjures up visions of wool rolling off with nice even strokes of the shears; and the money rolling in from the federal wool incentive. Nothing like what really happens when I shear the sheep.

When I shear sheep everything rolls but the wool. It's just like Saturday night wrestling, except for the ropes. I use more ropes.

If I had a partner to tag, and could jump off the turnbuckle to catch the sheep, it would be just like the Main Event. And if a sheep could shout into a microphone, they would sound smarter than those guys on TV.

You will also notice I use the generic term "sheep," which can mean one or a thousand. Folks often assume we have a whole bunch, but the truth is my son's flock has been reduced to one ewe and her lambs.

I mentioned this last summer to the editor of a national sheep magazine, and he got a big laugh out of it. He agreed that one sheep is pretty easy to keep track of.

For those who are crazy enough to shear their own sheep, a Canadian sheepman gives some excellent advice in a recent column for Grainews published in Winnipeg. He suggests those who want to try shearing their own should wait until late spring, when the wool has a natural break next to the skin. The sheepman emphasizes the importance of sharp shearing equipment.

He suggests learning the proper shearing strokes, rather than what he describes as the "Canadian shearing method," which consists of making a white spot on the sheep and then making it larger until the wool is all off.

This reminded me of my first attempt at shearing. I had brand new shears with sharp cutters when I began. But by the time I finished, the shears were old and the cutters dull; I don't think I've had a sharp piece of equipment since.

Those old ewes had plenty of breaks in the wool by the time I got done with them. I think they would have pulled their fleeces off and handed them to me if they could.

And I always wait until late spring and after lambing to shear the ewes. I used to postpone the job until the lambs could survive on their own if necessary, but I've learned I'm not quite that dangerous.

Of course everyone knows the best way to shear sheep is to hire a professional to come in and do the job. I've thought about that, but I keep having this vision of a shearer setting up all of his equipment and then asking, "How many do you have?"

Porch Stories

Every family has its stories, handed down through the generations like an old rocker. Like the chair, the stories have been sanded and varnished, but the original framework remains intact.

Family stories are artifacts of the era when folks sat on the porch and visited — before television destroyed such forms of entertainment. Telling stories was an art form in the days before TV.

My Dad and uncles are famous for stories. When I was a kid, they would sit on the porch for hours, staring into the darkness and retelling an old story that most of us had heard 20 or 30 times.

No one objected to hearing these fables repeated though, because you never really heard the same story twice. Something new was added with each telling until the story seemed to have a life of its own. Accuracy is irrelevant to a good story-teller.

So Dad would tell the story about Rusty Gates riding his bike down the gravel road past Uncle Dale's farm, and everyone would laugh as if they had never heard it before. Then each person would try to add something to it, making the story a little better the next time around.

To enjoy the Rusty Gates story, you have to understand that my uncle's farm was near the bottom of a steep hill, and his front yard was bordered by a tall hedge. Uncle Dale happened to be out trimming the hedge the day Rusty came riding by.

This was in the early days of automobiles, and people who didn't have cars often travelled on bicycles. Rusty Gates was a big, lanky kid about 20 years of age. On this particular day he was heaven-bent for somewhere.

The pedals were just a-flyin' when Rusty crested the hill, as the story goes, and he must have been doing 40 miles an hour when he reached the bottom of the grade. Then, suddenly the old bike hit a patch of gravel and Rusty went crashing headlong through Uncle Dale's hedge fence.

Although he wasn't hurt, dust and twigs were still falling when Rusty and his bike came to rest next to the flowerbed. He was as surprised to see someone in the yard as Uncle Dale was to see someone flying through the hedge.

"Where in the world are you going, Rusty?" Uncle Dale asked in surprise.

"Well, I thought I was going to visit my sister in Jackson Center," Rusty stammered.

Then everyone would laugh as if that was the funniest thing they ever heard, and someone would start on another favorite.

As I look back, there were two things that destroyed the art of story telling. TV was one of them, but the demise of the front porch was the other.

The modern home may have a deck or a patio, but somehow these just can't replace a porch. It was best described by the old man who went to visit his son, and was served lunch on the patio — on a day when the flies and mosquitoes were something ferocious.

"Son," the old guy said, "this is the darnedest thing. We used to eat in the house and go to the bathroom outside, and now you folks have just turned the whole thing around."

The Beagle Brigade

It's always interesting to see how various agencies react to a problem. When the FBI wants to catch drug smugglers they bring out their helicopters and speed boats and put a mean-looking German shepherd in the airport to sniff luggage for contraband.

But when the Department of Agriculture wants to prevent undeclared food and plants from entering the country through airports, they trot out a little beagle in a green coat and call him the Beagle Brigade. It's all part of a person's upbringing I guess; anyone who grew up on a farm would rather hunt anything with a beagle than a German shepherd.

The U.S.D.A. started the Beagle Brigade in 1986 and has since expanded it to seven international airports. When it comes to food, you can be sure nothing is getting by those little hounds.

The Beagle Brigade is supposed to sniff luggage, but these dogs aren't trained to find drugs. If you've ever owned a beagle, you know they aren't trained to do anything they didn't plan to do in the first place.

The FBI probably wouldn't understand this, but beagles are the ideal breed of dog for government service. Unlike a German shepherd or a doberman, a beagle is always polite; and when it comes to dedication to duty these little dogs are unsurpassed.

They're not very smart, but terribly dedicated. My first beagle, Gus, is a case in point; or maybe I should say was a case in point.

Gus is no longer with us, because he tried to run down a milk truck. Old Gus had developed a habit the houndog men call "cutting across." Once he got on the scent of a rabbit Gus would start taking out the zigs and zags by leaving the trail at a zig and cutting across to the next zag.

It saved a lot of distance and tended to straighten a rabbit out in a hurry. But Gus tried it on the milk truck and found they don't zag as much as a rabbit.

Smokey was my second beagle, and he was the most dedicated. We first took him hunting when he was about four months old, and just slightly bigger than the rabbits. Smokey would go under a big brush pile and howl at the rabbits until they couldn't stand the noise anymore.

If one of those rabbits had turned on him I don't know what he would have done. My brother and I used to worry that Smokey might run into a badger or a rabbit gang in one of those brush piles and have to fight his way out.

I mention Smokey because he had such a good nose and a terrific imagination. He would have been perfect for the Beagle Brigade.

That dog could pretend to be anything. If you gave him a little green coat he would probably sniff suitcases till the cows come home. And if you gave him a shovel and a hat, I think Smokey would have stomped out forest fires.

Steel-Toed Shoes

One of the fun things about writing a news column is that I get to read a lot of newspapers. Not just the big dailies like most people read, but a real variety of community newspapers as well as some excellent agricultural publications.

It keeps me in touch with the hinterlands, or at least I hope it does. One of the newspapers I enjoy is the Oakland-Hindsboro (Illinois) Prairie Sun.

The Prairie Sun isn't a big paper. It just covers the local news, school events, and tells how folks are doing — the most important functions of all community papers.

That's the strength of a rural community: People caring about each other — and about what's happening in their area.

The Prairie Sun devotes much of the back page to business ads. I would suppose the business owners buy this space, but instead of just advertising products they use it to report on whatever strikes their fancy.

They write about the soybean market, how Grandpa is doing in Florida, or what's likely to happen in this world if folks don't change their ways.

Good honest stuff and interesting reading. I'd hate to compete with some of those guys if they had as much time to write as I do.

This spring the machinery dealer wrote in the Prairie Sun, "Sunday sure was a different day from a week ago with temperatures almost 80. Probably gave some people garden fever.

"Vivian took care of my garden fever. Made me cut it down from the size of a big room to a small bathroom. Won't have to get in it to hoe. Can just stand around the edges."

The grain company wrote, "The corn and bean markets have been doing `their thing' the last few weeks. We are told that we have what's called a demand market. Once the weather fairs up and the corn gets planted we will find out how much demand we really have. Don't hold your breath for a big break — you might turn very purple!"

The machine shop owner writes, "Dropped an acetylene bottle off the back of a truck Friday and it landed right on my big toe. I was standing on concrete so that made it a professional job. Broke in two places and looked bad, but Dr. Bajaj got it fixed up and the Lord gave me a promise in Ecclesiastes 3:3 that states there is a `time to heal'."

The shop owner concludes with, "Don't forget Bible Preaching Meeting on Monday, April 30." And, "Get Some Steel Toed Shoes!"

I like these kinds of stories. They are short, full of personal experience, and between-the-lines, loaded with good humor and suspense.

When I read the machine shop item it brought back memories of the fellow who ran the repair shop in my old home town. He could fix a mowing machine sickle-bar almost as fast as I could break one.

I'm here to tell you, though, if old Fred had dropped the acetylene tank on his big toe, you couldn't repeat his comments at any Bible Preaching Meeting.

Keeping In Style

Keeping in style has always been a problem for me. Every time I buy a pair of wing-tip shoes or a big wide tie, someone decides they are out of style and I have to give them to the Salvation Army.

Most people don't realize the Salvation Army sets the styles in this country. If you go down there and look around, you'll see they're just a couple of years ahead of everybody else when it comes to clothing designs.

They know what's going to be in style, because they get first dibs on the stuff everybody else is throwing away. If a guy wants to ride the cutting edge of fashion, he should check with those fellows first.

Double-breasted suits are a good example. I saw a fashion article this week explaining that double-breasted suits are back in style, and they're not just for gangsters anymore.

The article says many men once considered these suits too flashy, but now anyone can look silly if they want to. The news article is accompanied by a photo of a model wearing a double breasted suit and leaning forward as if he is waiting for a bus, or has just been hit in the back with an ironing board.

The model is showing how neat and trim a man looks in a double-breasted suit. He looks like Stan Laurel does just after Ollie conks him with a two-by-four.

The model in the photo is stunning, and I know very well you could have gone to the Salvation Army store and bought that suit anytime during the last forty years. I know that because I used to own one, and it went to town in a big, plastic bag back in the early '70s.

I got my double-breasted for high school graduation and it was out of style before I got off the stage with my diploma. Those suits went out of style so fast it was hardly worth the trouble of buttoning them up.

But they came back just as fast and were in fashion again when I was a senior in college. This was fine with me; I never wore a suit unless I was graduating from something, anyway.

Now, the double-breasted is in again, and the designers are hoping we'll all go out and buy a new one. I don't think they'll get me this time.

I'm not graduating from anything; and if I was, I'll bet I could go down to the Salvation Army and get the same suit I wore twenty-five years ago.

Besides, I got into Western style clothes a number of years back. With this attire you can wear the same thing the cowboys wore 100 years ago. Western duds never go out of style.

With these clothes you don't have to look like a gangster, or a college professor or anything that might get you into a lot of trouble. My wife thinks my Western garb looks a bit too country when we go to the city; but I just tell folks I've been out herding sheep and am on my way home to change my clothes.

Run For Your Life
It's A Camera

The old saying that children should be seen but not heard is being tested by the increasing popularity of video cameras. It's getting so a kid can hardly turn around without winding up on video tape. I'm afraid we might end up with an entire generation of amateur actors.

I'm not sure all of this attention is good for a kid. I have always figured kids will show off enough without someone standing around encouraging them.

Family reunions are probably the worst. Some families just open the car door and out jumps Rin Tin Tin and a bunch of child stars. It's getting to the point where you can't have a picnic without a producer and some stage hands.

The kids seem to take it in stride though. They've been watching television since they could sit up, and being on film seems like a natural part of life for them.

It wasn't that way when I was a kid. Kids hated cameras in those days, and nobody despised having his picture taken more than I did.

If I saw someone headed my way with a camera, the photo came back as nothing but a cloud of dust on the horizon. You couldn't tell if it was me on a bicycle or the Jesse James Gang leaving the station. Like other primitive people, I was afraid the camera would capture my spirit.

In those days parents were pretty frugal with their film purchases, and we were lucky the cameras were generally out of focus. Most families have a few shots of a nude on a blanket, but no one can tell which kid it is.

These new video cameras are different, though. When Grandpa gets a Camcorder, a kid can look forward to having the rest of his life on tape.

The kids aren't the only ones to suffer from this filming. You have to feel sorry for friends and relatives that have to watch the tapes. I can't speak for others, but it only takes one episode of "Baby Eats Her Bananas" to convince me it's about time to go home.

My wife on the other hand is much more tolerant. She watches videos for hours at a time or until she gets motion-sickness, whichever comes first.

Connie was watching her sister's videos a few years ago when she suddenly realized the room was going in circles. The subjects weren't that bad, but constant movement of the camera made the viewer feel like a spider in a toilet bowl.

Last summer she tried it again and had to crawl out of the room after watching eight innings of little league baseball, two dance recitals, and a cat-washing. It was like watching "Spanky's Gang" from inside a clothes dryer.

Connie said, "You should sit down and watch your niece tap dance. She is really talented!"

"No thanks," I said. "If I want to get sick, I'll just load up the washing machine and watch the spin cycle."

Who's Counting?

"Don't tell them about the hole in the ribs, or the one in the shoulder. We'll tell the other guys you shot him in the head," I advised.

My son's deer had a hole in the head all right, and I could see no reason to dwell on the other details. Besides, I was hoping that if I kept my mouth shut about his shooting, the boy might quit telling people about the time I ran out of cartridges and still didn't get the deer I was shooting at.

"Those other guys are going to tell you all kinds of stories. You don't have to tell them how many times you shot at the deer," I continued.

"Those were pretty long shots from where I was sitting. How far away do you suppose I was?" Russell asked.

"Oh, hundreds of yards, at least," I said. "You were just as far away as you want to be. When the other guys tell you they shot their deer at 300 yards, you just tell them yours was running full speed, and you shot him in the head."

When we got back to the road a friend said two hunters had

come by with a three-point, but it was a lot smaller than my son's fork-horn. Later that day we saw the hunters who bagged the three-point, and they claimed it was the biggest three-point deer they had ever seen.

It's a hard lesson for a young hunter to learn those old guys don't always tell the truth; but a fellow is going to find them out sooner or later.

I'm getting so I never return from hunting without a full load of stories. There's no sense in being unprepared when you have to face the other hunters.

Some folks think hunters and fishermen always exaggerate and claim more success than they actually had; but that's missing the point of these stories.

It's not important to bag more game or catch more fish than the other guy. What's important is that you don't let his story top yours.

I told my son about the time my brother Kenny and I were hunting rabbits, when I was a teen-ager. We had a pretty good morning and were near our limits when we stopped at a truck stop for lunch.

An older hunter from our area was at the cafe and approached our table to talk about hunting. The first thing he said was, "We were only out for an hour or so. All we got was a couple of pheasants. How'd you guys do?"

"Oh, we didn't get anything," Kenny replied.

After the older man left, I asked my brother, "Why didn't you tell him about the rabbits we shot?"

Kenny said, "I knew he didn't have two pheasants, and figured if he was going to lie to us, why should I tell him the truth?"

Land Use Planning

I had to chuckle at a recent magazine column by Jon Bowerman of Fossil, Oregon in which he describes the concerns of landowners about national scenic river designations. Jon is a rancher, poet, and writer with a knack for getting to the meat of things without dripping blood all over the place.

He explains the days before land use planning when, "Folks just naturally seemed to do what common sense told 'em was best. They put the stockyards and the dump downwind from town. They built the sheriff's office and jail across the street from the saloon and the bank. On the upper end of town, where it was peaceful and quiet, they built the church, school, and cemetery."

But now we have land use planners, and I think Jon and I would agree the planners don't locate the outhouses any better than the old-timers did. I wouldn't go so far as to say a certain amount of government planning isn't needed, but I generally trust the landowners further than I do the government.

I remember attending a grain marketing conference in

Chicago back in the '70s when land use planning was still cutting its teeth in many rural areas. We had lunch on the 66th floor of the Sears building and looked out over thousands of acres of the best corn ground in the world — all covered with freeways and houses as the Chicago suburbs oozed into the cornbelt.

My thoughts were on the agricultural land in my home county and the efforts to save this land from housing and development. I thought of my own house settled on eight acres of jack pines which grow on that special class of land called "scab ground" in this part of the country. I recalled my conversation with a man from North Carolina a few years earlier in which I described my property as pines and "scabland." My North Carolina friend said, "Ah think thet's about the most descriptive term Ah've ever heard."

Standing there on the 66th floor of the Sears building I thought, "Why are we so worried about protecting land that never produced 40 bushels of grain the best year of its life, while cities like Chicago continue to devour the best cropland in the world?"

I was reminded of an old friend in the East who wanted to sell five acres of rocks and gullies for someone to build a house on. The five acres happened to be directly across the road from a neighbor who was on the zoning board and didn't want another house that close to him. The zoning variance was denied because the land was in an agricultural zone, and housing isn't an agricultural use.

My friend doesn't take such things lightly. So he found an old rusty combine and dragged it down to the five acre field across from his neighbor's house. Then he found an old corn picker, some wagons, and a few other items for decorating that little hillside.

Now the neighbor watches the sun rise over one of the country's largest and most informal collections of old agricultural machinery.

Frank (not his real name) told the neighbor, "OK, that's agricultural land and this is agricultural machinery; and when this stuff rusts away, I know where there's a lot more."

Lean and Hungry

It's always interesting to compare American farming practices with those of other countries. Such comparisons aren't always valid, but it is interesting nonetheless.

This occurred to me several years ago as I was standing in a hotel in France talking with some farmers from Pennsylvania about the dairy farms in England. Never mind that I don't know anything about dairy farms in England; but it just happens that the guys from Pennsylvania were the only people in the hotel I could understand.

The tour guide got me into the conversation because she doesn't know siccum about farms and had the uncertain notion that maybe I did. The Pennsylvania dairymen couldn't understand why the farm they visited in England seemed to be 20 years behind what we are doing in this country. They said things were dirty, the equipment was outdated, and the cows didn't look too good either.

I couldn't say much because I hadn't visited the English dairy, but I suspect their tour guide simply took them to the wrong farm. I'm sure they're not all the same.

This idea surfaced again recently as I was reading a news report of two U.S. chicken magnates (poultry farmers) visiting a Soviet poultry complex. The article reports the U.S. poultrymen found the Russian birds to be "lean and narrow-breasted." Not the type Colonel Sanders made famous.

When you consider the Soviets' reputation for showing only their best farms you can bet there are some thin yard-birds out in the countryside. I'll wager they have poultry that can run through chicken wire without breaking stride.

I know about such things because we had chickens like that when I was a kid. It wasn't a lack of feed, either. These chickens grew tough from an abundance of exercise.

In the old style of poultry production the birds had a lot of freedom, but they also had a certain amount of responsibility. They got fed on a regular basis and the rest of the time they chased grasshoppers, mice, snakes — whatever they could get.

Then, when these wild and woolly chickens got big enough to eat, we would chop their heads off and they would run around the yard with great abandon. Some folks think that's better than modern poultry production methods, but it's hard to get a chicken's viewpoint on this.

We visited a German farm on the same European tour I mentioned at the beginning of this column. This farmer kept all of his cows and calves in the barn year-around, and while the farm was a bit old-fashioned by U.S. standards, the animals seemed happy enough.

Several members of our group were horrified that the German farmer's cows weren't allowed out of the barn, and commented to this effect as we boarded the bus.

Just down the road I noticed a neighboring German farm where cows stood in the mud and rain, their backs hunched-up against the March wind. I commented to a lady across the aisle of the tour bus, "If I were a cow, I think I'd rather be in the barn."

The Winning Edge

I think the hardest thing to teach your kids is the importance of being competitive. No matter how much you pound it into them, many kids just won't accept the concept that all of life is a competition; and the person who has the most things when he dies is the winner.

You can see it in sports, and you can see it in other contests: Kids today just don't have the competitive desire their parents would like to see.

I guess I notice it most at junior livestock shows, where we have kids raising animals and taking them to the County Fair in the hope of having the Grand Champion and winning a trophy, or eating a bunch of cotton candy, or squirting water at each other.

Some of these kids have the winning edge and some of them don't. I've learned over the years that my kids would be happy to win something, but they aren't going to get into a big sweat about it.

This is hard for me to understand — because I am such a

competitive person. My first year in FFA, I showed a dairy heifer at the County Fair and took second place in a class of two animals. That was just the beginning for me.

The following year I had a corn project and exhibited three stalks at the Fair. That was even more fun!

Some folks may not think exhibiting three stalks of corn is exciting; but it is if you are a sophomore in high school, and the Fair gives you a season pass for bringing in the corn.

All exhibitors got a season pass in those days. The pass got you in free and entitled you to stay on the grounds overnight to take care of your exhibit. You'll have to admit — a kid with three stalks of corn has a pretty heavy responsibility.

So I stayed overnight to watch my corn, and hopefully soak up some of the culture that abounds on a fairgrounds.

I soon learned that corn is a lot more fun to show than livestock. You don't have to feed it, and it pretty much takes care of itself once you get it to the Fair.

My friends and I stayed overnight in the sheet-metal tent. The tent wasn't made of sheet-metal, but the company that owned it installed furnaces and did other kinds of metal work.

We boys spent the night watching after the furnaces on exhibit in the tent. You never know when someone will try to break into a tent and steal a furnace in the middle of July.

But we had a good time at the Fair and I got a ribbon for my corn, although I can't remember what sort of ribbon it was. That fall I sold the production from my six-acre corn project and bought a shotgun with the profits.

I've always tried to encourage my kids to get involved in sports and livestock shows and other sorts of competitions. Sometimes they're not as competitive as I would like.

It's enough to make a person wonder: Is this kind of thing hereditary?

The Harvest Gene

There's something about harvest season that affects each person differently. I'm not sure I can explain it for everyone, but farmers understand what I mean.

For many it's a sort of trance, in which nothing else matters until the crop is in the bin. These people speak quickly, make snap decisions, and leap small buildings in their haste to get the crop out before rain, frost, or relatives arrive.

Others take a laissez faire attitude, sipping coffee and talking slowly as if they don't have a worry in the world — all the while twisting their napkin and watching the clouds through the window.

I have never been a farmer, but I must have inherited the harvest gene from my ancestors. It shows up when I take the family to pick berries.

When I see ripe fruit my hands start to sweat, my eyes glass-over, and I start yelling for someone to bring the truck. It's food, I figure, and if we don't get it the bears will.

I look at a big field of huckleberries and wonder if we should open it up from the edges, or start with a swath down the middle. I wish for better equipment and lament how much faster this would be if my berry can were bigger.

Next I check for ripeness and chew a few berries between my teeth the way the wheatgrowers do. I worry about rain and the chance a big bear will come by and eat the whole crop before I can get my laborers into the field.

I cuss the bureaucrats who say my kids are too young to pick berries, and the child psychologists who say I shouldn't make them.

The wife and kids, on the other hand, can't seem to identify with harvesting food. When they think of food, they envision a supermarket.

My kids go berry picking with all the enthusiasm of slaves traveling to America. It seems everyone has a good excuse not to go.

It's all part of a person's upbringing, I think. Whereas my family comes from a long line of farmers and merchants, my wife descends from doctors and coal miners. While I'm crawling through bushes harvesting food at a fraction of the retail price, she's treating abrasions and forming a union.

The kids make light of berry picking. They laugh and throw fruit at each other. When I was a kid this sort of behavior would draw threats from my oldest brother, who would offer to throw kids at each other.

I believe my attitudes come from the childhood environment and my farming ancestors. My wife thinks these traits stem from more distant folks, the hunters and gatherers.

She may have a point there. I can close my eyes and see my ancestors dressed in skins and running after a hairy mammoth.

Uncle Ott is there, and he's shouting, "Get the gate! Get the gate! For God's sake can't anybody get the gate?"

Holiday Traditions

Those who cherish their holiday traditions will be happy to learn the old-fashioned celebrations are alive and well. The expectation that families will get together and eat a turkey the size of a St. Bernard remains deeply ingrained in the American conscience.

I don't know who decided everyone should eat a big turkey and a quart of cranberries for Thanksgiving, but they surely put the rest of us under a lot of pressure. I'm not suggesting traditions aren't important, but a smaller bird or maybe a roast would do just as well.

The best Thanksgiving meal I can remember was a salmon, but they wouldn't let me have one this year. There's nothing wrong with turkey, but I already had the fish.

When I think back on it, I suspect the Pilgrims had problems with their first Thanksgiving dinner, too. History tells us the Pilgrims envisioned this event as a time for giving and celebrating new friendships.

So they invited the Mohawks over and gave them smallpox.

In return, the Pilgrims got Manhattan Island, and had to eat leftover turkey for several weeks.

After this shaky start, Thanksgiving became a "family day." This reduced the risk of disease transmission, and gave the Puritans a chance to preach to each other — a tradition families have maintained over all these years.

As the celebration grew, so did families. By the early 1800s, families had so many kids that inviting everyone to Grandma's house was the only way to get a good count. This was the beginning of our modern day tradition.

More recently the big-turkey/big-family thing has become the bane of holiday celebrations. Birth control has made the problem worse. How can you eat a big turkey dinner and all the trimmings if you only have two kids?

The sociologists tell us Grandmas have changed, too. Many are tired of cooking and washing dishes for two days, only to see the same people for whom they cooked and washed the past thirty years.

Some Grandmas respond frankly, "You can go `Over the river and through the woods' if you want, but I'm gonna be in Florida!"

Into this caldron of tradition steps the modern mother, who has worked all week to keep food on the table and credit cards in her purse — but still remembers the days when Grandma cooked a big turkey with all the trimmings every Thanksgiving.

Torn between the old and the new, modern woman buys the biggest bird she can find and she's going to roast it, come drought or high taxes. I'm not saying there's anything wrong with that.

I'm just asking, "Can we please have ham for Christmas?"

A Mother Never Forgets

The sport of fishing has taken on new meaning with all of the new-fangled equipment one can buy these days. Traditionally a sport of the masses, fishing now offers so many expensive gadgets that even the rich can enjoy themselves.

A lot of water has passed under the boat since the day I walked boldly into the hardware store to buy my first flyrod, a nice little eight-footer with just the right balance and action to cast a bluegill fly. I assumed my rod was of ideal weight and length for the fishing I had in mind — it was the only flyrod they had in the store, anyway.

Then, I selected a reel with an automatic retrieve, a roll of E-level line, and a few woolly, little flies with a gold bead on the head. I've often thought back to that day with the fond assurance that was the worst conglomeration of fishing equipment a young boy has ever been saddled with.

I wish I could remember if the store had more than one reel and one spool of flyline, or if they carried any flies without weighted heads. But a young boy has no time to quibble. When he needs equipment, he needs equipment!

By the time I learned (a year or two later) that the line was several sizes too light for the rod, I had beaten those little beady flies into oblivion and scared the feathers off countless shore birds.

Casting that E line was like throwing a spider web into the wind, and those automatic reels had about as much finesse as a runaway window-blind.

Just about the time I had tamed the flyrod to the point I could catch a fish once in while, I realized my main problem wasn't presentation — my problem was getting to the fish.

So I went down to the army surplus store and bought an inflatable boat, one of those four-man models about the size of a small bathtub. Now I was set for some serious fishing.

On my first trip I inflated the boat with my bicycle pump and headed out into the lake for some fishing. I was out only a few minutes and had caught a nice crappie when I noticed the boat was getting smaller.

Sensing a wet rear-end in my future, I began rowing for shore. By the time I neared shore the boat was closing in, giving me and my craft the bizarre appearance of a hot-dog rowing a bun. With leaks at both oarlocks, the boat was never repaired.

All of this came back to me recently as I was telling my mother about my son's new float-tube and its reputed ability to get a person to the fish. "We thought about buying a canoe," I told her, "but decided float-tubes might be just the thing for fishing the small lakes."

"Well, I hope it isn't like the rubber boat you bought when you were his age," she laughed.

Isn't that a mother for you. Some people never forget!

How To Read A Worm

Summer's barely over and already folks are predicting a hard winter. There's something about winter that leads to pessimism. I've found that predictions of hard winters outnumber soft winters by six to one.

That's because most people base their predictions on faulty information. They look at the wrong indicators.

For example, the woolly worm is still the most reliable indicator of a hard winter. But you can't go by its color as most people think.

The old wives tale that a black woolly worm suggests a hard winter goes back to the days when people had old wives, and heated with coal. Everytime someone went out to the coal bin they'd find a black woolly worm. They just naturally assumed cold weather had something to do with it.

A woolly worm is still a good predictor if he's used right. But the way to read one of these fuzzy beasts is to stand back and watch which direction he's going.

If the worm is headed south, it's going to be a hard winter.

If he's going north it may be spring already and you might want to take him fishing. A worm heading south and carrying a sleeping bag means you should get into the house quickly before your nose freezes.

A woolly worm going in circles is a real bad sign. This means you are in the middle of a tornado and cold weather should be the least of your concerns.

There are many false prophets in the weather prediction game. Long hair on the horses means nothing in terms of weather. It just means the horse has worms.

A squirrel storing nuts in August tells us little. This is likely a young squirrel who starts school in September.

A better indicator of bad weather is the amount of hair on the polar bears. Anytime you see a big, hairy polar bear, it's almost sure to be a hard winter.

Last fall I read an article in which a wildlife biologist said he didn't believe animals could predict the weather. He said wild critters develop behavior patterns that help them survive, and then pass these behaviors to future generations.

He concludes the color pattern on a woolly worm is probably due to genetic variations, and has nothing to do with the weather. The same color combinations are found every year, he said.

I don't know about genetics in woolly worms, but I suppose we could relate this to people. There is good evidence that cold weather can increase genetic variation in humans.

Anthropologists will confirm that any place you find lots of kids and a great amount of genetic variation, you can bet these folks have had a lot of long, cold winters.

Hogs Loading At Gate 6

The airlines have revolutionized the way people travel these days. A person can get on a plane in Chicago and be nearly anywhere in a few hours. It would be more fun if they could tell you where you're going, but I'm always so glad to get out of Chicago I don't even ask.

On my last trip through that part of the country I learned the Chicago airport has installed one of those people conveyers like they have in London (and a bunch of other places I don't know much about). A person just climbs aboard this moving belt and the conveyer delivers him to the other end of the terminal, looking and feeling just like a sack of potatoes.

This summer, my wife and I boarded this contraption near gate C-14 in a mad rush to get to our next flight at gate B-24. When we arrived at B-24 the desk clerk announced our flight had been moved to gate C-16. So we got back on the conveyer and headed back where we came from.

That's how the big airlines keep their passengers alert and on edge so they won't think too much about what this trip is costing them. The little airlines are a bit different, but they keep the passengers on their toes, too.

I took my first trip on a small commuter plane a couple of years ago and was amazed at the difference between commuter air travel and flights on the larger planes.

Things are much less formal on the smaller planes, and you don't have to arrive at the airport an hour early. They board commuter planes just before take off, much like we loaded hogs when I was a kid.

We always tried to get hogs on the truck and then take off as fast as possible so the pigs wouldn't get to fighting; and that's exactly the way the commuter planes do it. We also sprayed the hogs with water to cool them down, but the airlines don't generally resort to that.

I can see why the passengers might get to fighting on these smaller planes. A person boards at the front and then walks hunched-over toward the back of the plane, until he finds a seat.

Then, if a guy draws the seat at the rear, he's likely to be wedged between two more passengers who are pretty near market weight. What's worse, the small planes don't have that feeling of security one senses on the big airliners.

Readers may have heard about the commuter plane that lost an engine over the Gulf. The pilot was calm as could be when he told the passengers, "Well folks, it looks like we are in for some real trouble this time. Is there anyone on this plane who knows how to pray?"

A guy in the back raised his hand and shouted, "Yes, Brother, I sure do!"

The pilot said, "That's good, 'cause we don't have enough parachutes for everyone."

The Racing Bed

Every community needs a celebration. Whether it's a "Harvest Festival", "Schnitzel Week", or "Community Daze", every burg should have something to celebrate.

I think the hardest thing in planning a celebration is coming up with some games. You can only run around with one leg in a sack for so long, before the whole thing gets tedious.

One of the most popular contests for community celebrations these days is the bedrace. There's something about a bedrace that makes it sound exciting.

"Bedrace" has a nice ring to it and people will come out to see a contest like that. This event sounds especially exciting to the person who doesn't have the slightest idea what it is.

For those who have never seen one, a bedrace is a test of speed — requiring a bed on wheels, four people to push it, and someone to ride in the bed. The person in the bed is often a young lady — of the approximately the same weight as a sack of potatoes.

The object is to arrive at the finish with the bed and its

occupant before any of the other teams.

Conconully, Washington has an outhouse race based upon similar principles; but this contest just doesn't have a fun ring to it. To me an outhouse race sounds more desperate than anything else.

My only experience with a bedrace was a number of years ago, when I was appointed chairman of the fraternity bedrace committee. The brothers assigned me and two agricultural engineers to build a bed for the May Day race around "The Oval" of the Ohio State University campus.

If you have never seen a racing bed built by a farm kid and two agricultural engineers, you can't imagine what we tried to push around the oval. We probably could have built a pretty good hay feeder, but beds on wheels were completely out of our field.

When I look back on that experience, I can see that our bed was probably more like a hay feeder than anything else. It had two wheels on the back, mounted to a wooden frame; and one wheel on the front which could be turned for easy cornering. I'll bet the whole thing didn't weigh more than 1,000 pounds.

But we wheeled it out for the race, confident that if we didn't finish well on May Day, we could still use the thing for a hay feeder the following winter.

Then, we got Don Long's fiancee to ride in the bed, because she was the only girl we knew who had courage enough to do such a thing. We got two-thirds of the way around the track before the front wheel fell off our racing bed.

A lot of folks will tell you that the most important thing a person can learn in college is where to find information on a subject of interest. That's the way I look at this bedrace experience.

If this had been an outhouse race, I think we could have won. The agricultural engineers on my committee had some really good plans for those.

One Man's Hurricane

I guess I'll never be an artistic person. I have little patience with the abstract and simply can't understand anything that doesn't look like something.

This may be true of most men who grew up on a farm. There were just so many old pieces of equipment and unusual things lying around when we were kids, that we suspect everything has a purpose if we can only find out what it is.

So I look at a metal sculpture and instead of seeing the broad, sweeping curves and graceful symmetry, I see the sharp edges and comment, "I'll bet that thing came off an old corn-chopper."

It's just that sort of attitude that causes problems when artists are commissioned to design pieces for public buildings on college campuses. What might have been an artistic triumph if placed in the college of art, looks like the rear end of a manure spreader when you put it near the dairy science building.

That's just what happened at Washington State University back in the '70s. The university had a huge metal sculpture placed next to the animal science building, and once the shock subsided everyone began to guess what it was.

Each time I visited that campus, I would look at this monstrosity and try to make something out of it. The piece had several sections of 12 to 15-foot lengths, and each was suspended at various angles to the ground.

After the sculpture was in place for a few months, the head of the animal science department became so curious that he offered a six-pack of beer for the person who could come up with the best name for it.

The winner was a professor who dubbed the piece "Hog Troughs in a Hurricane." And he was right! That's exactly what it looks like.

Probably the most intriguing art pieces for me are the natural arrangements of dried plants and flowers. Each time I look at a dried arrangement, I find myself identifying the plants it contains; and pretty soon I'm calculating the nutritive value of this mixture if fed to a sheep.

The first dried arrangement my wife put together was a beautiful combination of curly dock and timothy, arranged in a big moonshine jug. While these plants were attractive enough, I have seen too many of them encased in baling wire to understand why you would put them in a jug.

These bouquets always remind me of that wet spot in the hay field — where the weeds were so bad we didn't even bother to cut it. To this day, I have trouble walking past a dried arrangement without giving it a kick to see if a quail might fly out.

Such decorations have become big business, however, and there are farms with whole fields planted specifically for this market. They tell me the main concern in growing decorative plants is not climate or soil fertility: The biggest problem is keeping an eye on Grandpa to be sure he doesn't spray the weeds before you can get them off to market.

No Rest For The Guilty

Volunteers are still the backbone of America. When there's a barn to be built, a war to be fought, or festival organized, volunteers have never failed to shoulder the load.

People perform these duties because they want to — or know they would feel guilty if they didn't help out. It comes under community service: Community Days Committee, School Board, Kiwanis Club, Jaycees, Cemetery Cleanup Committee.

Volunteers have performed these jobs so successfully the courts are getting involved by assigning "community service" in lieu of other penalties. Readers may have noticed sentences like "$200 fine, six months probation, and 90 hours of community service." Apparently judges think community service time is useful experience for the offender as well as accomplishing good deeds around the community.

This is a bad idea in my opinion. Now we are punishing people by making them do things other folks have been doing for nothing all of these years. Before long we will have people committing crimes and claiming they did it because they enjoy serving their community.

Already we have folks who volunteer to avoid feeling guilty, working right next to those who really are guilty! I found myself in this situation last summer when I volunteered to dig a ditch at the county fairgrounds. Our county fair livestock arena is outdoors, and we needed to drain an area that had resembled a swamp for many years.

The county employees would have dug the ditch, but they were short of manpower, or a backhoe wasn't available; and the jail trustees they had working for them couldn't be trusted with a backhoe anyway. So I said "I'll bring my shovel and a wheelbarrow, and dig the @#*& %#@*$ ditch myself!"

You might say I volunteered. Then, I waited for the hottest day of the year and began digging. Before long the county fellows came by with a young man to help me dig. They said he was on "community service."

The boy was a good worker, and we got along fine. The county guys said this fellow didn't always work so hard, but we can surmise the kid was nervous about the guy working next to him.

I didn't ask the boy what he did to earn his community service, and he was afraid to ask about mine. Any kid who has clashed with the court system knows a guy sentenced to digging ditches in mid-summer has committed crimes normal folks can't even think about.

Finally the boy couldn't stand it any longer. "Do you work for the county?" he asked.

"No," I said.

"Is this your job? Do you just go around digging ditches?" he inquired.

"No." I replied.

"Then why are you doing it?"

I looked up from my shovel with the sweaty-eyed glare of a ditch digger and said, "I can't help it, kid. Every time I see a wet piece of ground, I just have this terrible urge to dig a ditch through it."

The Winner And Still Unconscious

I don't know what the exotic pet business is coming to. First it was llamas, then pot-bellied pigs, and now we have fainting goats.

Fainting goats are not new, I guess. According to what I've read they've been around for 100 years or so. Only recently have they gotten much press, however.

For those who haven't heard, fainting goats result from an inherited genetic disorder (myotomia congenita) that causes the animal's muscles to tense up when frightened. Something as innocent as a simple "Boo!", or a .44 magnum fired over their heads, will cause these goats to fold up like an accordion.

When the animal is frightened, its body becomes rigid for 10 to 15 seconds and then it gets up and walks away, apparently as good as new. Owners have said the condition would be much easier to deal with if anyone knew for sure what scares a goat.

My sources say the fainting condition was first noticed in a group of goats from Tennessee around the turn of the century. Once the goats' owners realized the condition was heritable, they began breeding these animals to protect other livestock, such as sheep, from predators.

The idea was for the goat to become frightened by the predator and keel-over. By the time the predator had finished with the goat, the sheep had escaped. (Just like the old "grizzly bear and the hunters" joke.)

That really doesn't sound good to me, but no one got upset about raising these animals until recently. If the owners hadn't become smitten with the urge to show-off to their neighbors there would be no controversy.

Like all livestock producers these goat owners wanted to prove their animals were the best. So they scheduled contests, with up to $1,000 in prize money for the goat that fainted quickest or stayed down the longest.

Obviously this was a bad idea. Who wants to attend a livestock show, where the Grand Champion may never get up?

Before anyone could rethink this contest idea, the animal rights activists started fainting. I don't know if it's genetic or not, but research has shown the only thing that gets excited faster than a goat is an animal rights activist. These folks say raising a goat just to watch it faint is a form of animal cruelty.

My customary policy of remaining impartial prevents me from criticizing these goat owners. There is good evidence that all goats carry a fainting gene to some extent. Generations of farm kids would attest that any goat will faint: It just takes more to scare some than others.

Before anyone gets too self-righteous I think we need to take a look in our own backyard. I've never owned a fainting sheep, but I've seen some consider it seriously.

Sometimes it's hard to be objective about our own pets, or to understand someone else's. If we are going to throw stones, I'm always going to remember the folks who raise cats just to watch them spit-up on the rug.

Put Up Hay With A Trebuchet

My wife found it in her car — a *Wall Street Journal* story about a man in England who built a full-sized replica of a trebuchet (pronounced tray-boo-shay). The trebuchet is a medieval siege engine, used by ancient armies for throwing dead horses and other unwanted items over castle walls during an attack. (A form of biological and psychological warfare.)

The news article explains that Hew Kennedy of Acton, England built this contraption so he could throw old pianos and dead animals around his pasture. When Earl Butts said western Oregon has more kooks per square mile than anywhere else, he apparently forgot about England.

How did the news story get into my wife's car? A friend put it there while Connie was at work. That's the difference between small towns and cities.

In the city, people take things out of your car; in the country, they put things into your car. Our friend saw the article about the trebuchet and thought, "Here's something Roger could use in his column."

Where would I be without my friends? When the conversation turns to mad men and dead horses, they always think of me. They bring me little treasures like a cat drags things to the doorstep.

"Hey, Sparkey! What do you have there? Oo-ooh it looks dead! Maybe Roger can use this in his column."

The news story says Mr. Kennedy built his trebuchet with a three-ton, 60-foot tapered beam. The wooden beam pivots on a steel axle and is attached at the heavy end to a box containing 5 $\frac{1}{2}$ tons of steel bar.

A steel cable is attached to the beam as a sling. The slinger prepares the trebuchet by pulling the beam down near the ground and hooking it to a substantial anchor. Then he attaches the sling cable to the slingee. When the beam is released, the slingee (rock, horse, piano) is hurled through the air like a spit-ball from a popsicle stick.

Medieval armies used horses to pull the beam to the ground, but Mr. Kennedy uses a tractor. I suspect the first trebuchets were made to throw rocks and pulled by a single horse. Using a horse that was too small led to the discovery that rocks might not be necessary.

Mr. Kennedy uses his trebuchet for throwing pianos, dead hogs, etc.; but he wonders, "Why couldn't a trebuchet be used commercially?"

That's why my friends brought the article to me. They figured I could find useful applications for a trebuchet in agriculture.

Putting hay bales in those old dairy barns leaps immediately to mind. Most barns have a big door at one end of the mow where loose hay or bales were once lifted on a hay fork. That was work, but kids would probably stand in line to put up hay with a trebuchet. (Makes a good slogan, too.)

Spreading manure is a natural, but requires some fine-tuning. Rounding up cows is stretching things a bit, but everyone has an old cow that always balks at the gate. The trebuchet would put her in the corral for good.

Mr. Kennedy reportedly offered his trebuchet to the movie directors of Robin Hood. He wanted them to use it in a scene where Kevin Costner and his buddy are catapulted over a wall.

That's probably the best use for the average farm: Aim it toward the road, hook it up to the salesman, and put a timer on it.

Artists Are Like Sheepherders

Public sponsorship of the arts has been under fire ever since folks realized many states require a percentage of the cost for new public construction must be spent for art — and that includes prisons. The public might tolerate a bust of Mickey Mouse in the courthouse, but they don't want to pay for a statue in the exercise yard.

I tend to agree. Not because I have anything against art or prisoners as we know them; but because I believe artists should fend for themselves rather than depend upon public money. The same goes for writers and poets.

There's something about art and writing that doesn't lend itself to public sponsorship. The idea that giving artists and writers public funding increases incentive is contrary to their personalities. These folks are like sheepherders: They have to be stone-cold broke before you can get any work out of them.

Like field mice, artists and writers are prone to over-population. If it weren't for poverty and editors there would be nothing to keep us in check.

The tradition of the starving artist has served our society well. If a person can't produce something people will buy with their own money, then starving is an apt conclusion.

I think the best example of a hungry artist is Charlie Russell. Charlie ran away from St. Louis as a kid and traveled west to become a cowboy.

There weren't any federal grants for cowboys in those days, so Charlie went to work on a ranch. If public sponsorship had been available, Charlie might have bought a pony and stayed in St. Louis, depriving the world of its greatest western artist.

Charlie didn't exactly starve during his years as a cowboy, but a steady diet of bacon and beans couldn't help but affect his cholesterol level. He lived in bunkhouses, tents, and tepees — all the while collecting material for his art. Charlie's pieces were flavored with the smoke of a campfire and dust of the trail.

Contrast this with what might have happened if the artist had a nice federal grant, instead of living on the open range. Charlie might have spent his best years holed-up in Helena, eating under a fern and negotiating with a committee for the arts.

He would have been miserable, and his art would have surely suffered. I shudder to think of the Western art that might have been lost in a situation like that.

Instead of pieces like "Bronc to Breakfast" and "Waiting For a Chinook", we might have had "Old Lady Eating Fern", or "Streets Plowed Often".

They can say what they want about public funding for art and all of that, but I'm convinced the world is a better place because Charlie and a lot of other artists had to fend for themselves.

Small Fields And Big Thinkers

I had almost forgotten what it was like — driving for hours on end without a radio and with no one to talk to. We used to do it on the old tractors, but nobody drives without a radio these days.

My daughter's car doesn't have a radio, and I had borrowed her automobile for a recent trip. It's amazing how much thinking a person can do while sailing down the freeway for several hours a day. It's just like driving the old tractors — nothing to do but think.

Laura's car doesn't have a radio because she can't afford the kind of speakers she wants. If she could spend a few days on a tractor without a radio she would have time to think about why she can't afford the car, either.

It gives me something to borrow, though, and I really like driving without a radio. When we were kids we drove those old tractors for hours on end, and a person really had time to think. A kid got in a lot of daydreaming during a summer on the tractor.

I should explain that daydreaming is to kids what thinking

is to adults. While the kids are daydreaming about fishing in Alaska or pitching a no-hitter, adults are thinking about what kind of a crop they might have and how they can pay for the combine.

If a guy has a big crop and the price is good, he could pay all of the bills and still have money left for a vacation. You can see this kind of thinking is just a more advanced form of daydreaming.

The main drawback to thinking while driving tractors is the effect it has on fences. We had small fields where I grew up, and a person had to keep his thoughts short or pay the consequences. More than one guy has wound up with his front wheels in the neighbor's soybeans because he let his thinking get the best of him.

All a guy can do then is fix the fence and try to smooth out the wheel tracks as best he can. You can stand the bean stalks back up, but they'll look pretty obvious.

Most people don't realize what working small fields can do to a person. People who grew up working short fields are afraid of big projects. A kid who never got more than ten minutes into a daydream will always be a bit conservative.

I can see it in my writing. If I get more than 1,500 words into anything, I have the feeling I should turn back, before I take out a fence or knock the corner off someone's barn. A person like that is always changing his mind.

Contrast this with folks who grew up in the big fields of Wyoming or Montana where they never have to turn around. These people think big, and they aren't easily discouraged. I'll bet there are people in those states who haven't changed their mind twice in their whole life.

Make It Be Good

There he was, 3-foot-7-inches tall, crouching-down at the plate, squeezing his little bat until sawdust dripped from the handle: Eddie Gaedel, the smallest player ever to play major league baseball.

A percentage of sports fans will remember Eddie Gaedel played in only one game, had one at-bat, and walked for the late Bill Veeck's St. Louis Browns. Gaedel was Veeck's answer to bad hitting.

The Browns were 46 games behind in the pennant race in 1951. Veeck thought it might be fun to bring in a little guy with a 3-inch strike zone, and then replace him with a pinch runner after he walked to first. It would give the fans a laugh and let them see someone get on base for a change.

So Veeck hired the late Eddie Gaedel, a 3-foot-7 midget and gave him a custom-made Browns uniform with the number "$1/8$" on the back. Eddie strolled to the plate with his 17-inch bat and walked on four pitches. Veeck reportedly threatened Eddie that if he so much as considered swinging at a pitch, Veeck would shoot him.

I was only seven years old when Eddie made his famous appearance in St. Louis, Missouri, but I saw the same thing five years later in St. Paris, Ohio. We didn't have any midgets in St. Paris, but we had little league, and I swear Eddie Gaedel's strike zone wasn't any smaller than Jeff Walters' (not his real name).

Jeff was nine years old and a Dodger the summer of 1956. I played for the Indians and our two teams were bitter rivals. Besides being small for his age, Jeff could crouch so low at the plate a lizard could have tapped him on the shoulder.

The Dodgers' bench must have threatened Jeff the same way Veeck threatened Gaedel. When he came to the plate, everyone on the bench would start hollering, "Make it be good, Jeff. Don't swing at any bad pitches!" Any little leaguer can tell you that means, "Swing at a pitch and you are dead meat!"

When I saw an old photo of Eddie Gaedel in the paper this week, I thought, "That's no midget. That's Jeff Walters when he was nine years old. Even the batting stance is the same."

Bill Veeck's little trick with Gaedel might not have worked if Johnny Bricker had been pitching for the opposition. Johnny was the only kid I ever saw strike out Jeff Walters.

Johnny was pitching for the Indians, and we were behind when Jeff Walters came to the plate. Jeff went into his batting stance like a banty hen snuggling down on her nest. Johnny squinted toward home trying to see a strike zone.

The count was three balls and no strikes, before a little curve dropped in for a strike. The next pitch squeezed through the strike zone as well, and the count was full.

Then Johnny did the unexpected. He served up a big, blooping change-up. Jeff started swinging when the pitch was half way to the plate, and was still flailing the air when the ball got to the catcher. We could have had three strikes on that one pitch.

Nobody could blame him. If any of us had been standing there watching pitches go by all summer, I think we would have done the same thing.

Corn, Cotton, And Cockleburs

"I come from a state that raises corn and cotton and cockleburs and Democrats, and frothy eloquence neither convinces nor satisfies me. I am from Missouri. You have got to show me."

Those famous words were spoken by Congressman Willard Vandiver of Cape Girardo, Missouri at a meeting in Philadelphia in 1889. One hundred years later few of us can remember what caused Willard's outburst, but his words still ring true for all who are forced to sit through meetings and conventions while thinking of the things they should be doing back home.

When a guy has a field full of corn and cockleburs and Democrats, he's in no mood for wasting his time at some political shindig. He wants to go home and get his crop cleaned-up.

I don't know if Congressman Vandiver was a farmer or not, but I'll wager he wiped the frothy eloquence off his boots more than once. Most of us would have liked Willard. He was a tough cookie.

When I think of Missouri I always think of corn and cotton and cockleburs and the "show me" philosophy espoused by the late congressman. His spirit lives in all who approach each year with the childlike expectation of a beautiful crop, tempered with the gnawing suspicion it might be a field full of cockleburs by summer.

A good example would be my friend Bonnie, who is quite a farmer in her own right and grows plants for artistic arrangements.

Last spring a friend gave Bonnie some seeds in a little brown package. She worked up a piece of her garden and planted them with great anticipation (and a little cow manure).

The seeds sprouted instantly and were soon transformed into neat rows of dark-green, broad-leaved plants. They grew like weeds and were expectant with bloom in no time at all.

Bonnie could envision the large beautiful flowers one might expect from such an interesting plant. Finally they bloomed and then formed seed pods, and then reality set in: Cockleburs! Two perfect rows of the nicest cockleburs you ever saw.

Bonnie didn't feel too bad though, because she remembered a friend whose father-in-law presented her with a package of mouse droppings which he claimed were flower seeds. Bev says the germination was so uneven there was hardly enough of a crop to feed the cats.

Now, you may be wondering about the moral to this story; and I've been wondering the same thing. As far as I can tell these experiences confirm what Congressman Vandiver said in Philadelphia in 1889, and what the agricultural colleges have recommended for a long time:

1. Don't buy the frothy eloquence.
2. Always have your soil tested.
3. And be sure to get certified seed!

Things That Go "Baa!" In The Night

It's hard for younger generations to appreciate the changes electricity brought to rural areas. Those who milked 30 cows by hand can tell us about it, but we can't fully understand.

Most of us will never experience the exhilaration of opening a feedbox and confronting a big, yellow cat with a coal oil lantern. (The farmer has the lantern.) Doing chores in the dark was just part of living, but that didn't make it any easier.

My Dad tells about a young man who walked down the road past Grandpa's farm to visit a neighbor before cars were common. This fellow was afraid of the dark, but would return after dusk some nights, carrying an old lantern and whistling to take his mind off the darkness.

Dad says the young fellow would be whistling softly and walking at a leisurely pace when he left the neighbor's; but by the time he traveled a mile or so the boy would be jogging along briskly and whistling at a much higher pitch. One night the lantern went out, and folks heard the young fellow pass in the darkness, whistling like a tea kettle and running 20 miles an hour.

I'm too young for coal oil lanterns (thank goodness), but I can remember when farms weren't lighted like they are today. We had lights, but they were all inside buildings and there weren't that many.

Adults didn't seem to mind the darkness between the house and the farm buildings, but the kids did. My brothers and I learned to scope out the path between the house and the barn before flipping any light switches.

One kid would hold the barn door open while the other flipped the switch. Then we would run like mad so nothing could catch us. We hid our fear by challenging each other to a race. If everyone's running anyway, we might as well call it a competition.

My scariest moments in the dark were when friends from town came to visit. Fear is contagious, and the town kids were afraid of everything. Of all the things they feared, being bitten was probably the worst.

Town kids would see a cow and ask, "Does she bite?" This seemed ridiculous to us. A person might get bitten by a dog, cat, or even a pig; but nobody gets gnawed by a cow.

The combination of cows and darkness really put these kids on edge. If we wanted to play basketball in the barn, we had to assure our guests there weren't any cows in there; or if there were they didn't have any teeth.

One dark and scary night my friend Willy and I decided to play some basketball in the hay mow. We got to the barn alright; but I could see Willy was getting nervous when I opened the door to the milking parlor.

Willy stuck with me like syrup on a pancake as I felt along the wall for the string to the light switch. Then, just as I reached for the light, something in the corner pen said "Baa!" Willy leaped through the barn door and was headed for the house before I could even turn around.

I wanted to tease Willy for being scared by a harmless little calf. I would have too, if I hadn't passed him three times between the barn and the back porch.

Futurists And Teenagers

This is the age of technology. So many things we learned to do as youngsters are now obsolete or performed by machines.

Even more disheartening is the thought that ethics and responsibilities drummed into us by our elders have somehow lost their value. This is what struck me a few days ago as I was preparing to clean a paintbrush.

All of my life I have thought it important to clean the brush when you finish painting. You are supposed to put the paintbrush in some paint thinner or gasoline and then work on it until it is nearly as good as new.

My wife, on the other hand, was raised in the belief that if you put a dirty brush in a soup-can full of gasoline, it will go away sooner or later.

It turns out she's right! Hers have all gone away. I thought about this a few minutes the other day and after putting my brush in a can with some paint thinner, I just threw the whole mess away.

In four days of painting I discarded six brushes. It was truly a liberating experience. Who am I to waste my time cleaning a paintbrush? Nobody else does.

When we were kids failure to clean a brush was on the route to financial ruin and caused severe wear on the seat of one's pants. I was taught that a person could expect to own only one good dog and one good paintbrush in a lifetime.

It hurts to admit it, but the new throw-away brushes have eliminated one of the few skills I was able to master as a youth. Now, you buy a little sponge on a stick to paint with and when you're done, you toss it in the trash.

The same day I threw the brushes away, I read about a "futurist" who says almost none of what kids are learning these days will be of any value a number of years down the road.

This caught my attention because it is exactly what my kids have been saying. There's really no point in learning history, or chemistry, or math when you are never going to see this stuff again.

It's fair to assume that the majority of high school students would agree with the futurist. On the other hand, test scores show many of these youngsters have nothing to worry about: They aren't learning enough about any of these subjects to hurt them in the long-run.

The futurists are saying we need to change our educational system and the outmoded values taught in the family. The world is changing so fast that what we learn today will be out-of-date tomorrow.

They say we shouldn't be learning to paint a boat and then clean the brush: The day is fast approaching when we will throw away the boat so we won't have to paint it.

Change is inevitable. When I was a kid, we didn't even have futurists. There were a few people sitting around predicting things — like the weather or how long it would be before the world exploded; but there weren't any bonafide futurists.

We did have teenagers, though; and as far as I can tell there's not a whole lot of difference.

It's The Pits

Farmers must tire of the question, "What do you do in the winter?" That's like asking Santa Claus, "What do you do in the summer?" Someone's gotta herd those @#&*# reindeer, you know.

There's plenty to do on a farm in the winter — especially when rain, snow, and mud add to the day's challenges. If you've ever crossed a muddy barnlot with a bucket of warm water in one hand and a bale of hay in the other, you know how good the warm water feels on one leg — compared to the freezing mud creeping up the other.

Farmers would probably like winter if it weren't for the mud and snow. On many farms, winter is the season for that ever-present mixture of mud and manure one university engineer has fondly labeled "shud."

Manure handling systems and concrete barnlots have reduced the shud problem on many farms, but there's still plenty of opportunity to get stuck. I will always remember an old friend who came to my office during the '70s with a safety booklet printed by the U.S. Department of Agriculture. We got a big laugh out of the booklet's effort to caution farmers with the warning, "Do not fall in the manure pits."

Nobody had manure pits when I was a kid. We used the whole farm.

The farm where I grew up had two barns: the "big barn" and the "hog barn." The big barn, with its hip roof and huge haymow, was used for feeding dairy cows and calves. The hog barn was much older and smaller. It housed the hogs, as you might expect.

When we sold the hogs and began feeding heifers in the old barn in later years, we had a problem with hay storage. Because the old barn didn't hold enough hay and straw for the entire winter, we had to carry bales across the muddy barnlot from the big barn to get it to the heifers.

Well, you can imagine how this worked in late winter. The barnlot would become soft and "mooshy" (as the kids would say), and anyone with less than six-inch tops on his boots was going to suffer some serious damage to his socks. Boots in those days were labeled as four-buckle and six-buckle. I can guarantee this was a six-buckle barnlot.

Our hay bales weighed about 70 pounds each. A 140-pound teenager carrying two bales of hay was close to 280 pounds of mass in size-eight boots.

Sinking below the tops of the boots was bad enough, but stepping out of a boot was even worse. If you weren't unshod and stuck in the shud by the time you got across the lot, you could be thankful for tall boots and quick feet.

I always think of muddy barnlots when I see today's teenagers walking around with their tennis shoes unlaced. I wonder if these kids have any idea how much shud a person could get in a $125 pair of Air Jordans if he doesn't lace them up.

Dadburn Gadgets

I don't think I will ever be comfortable in the city. The streets are confusing, the buildings are hard to identify, and even the people seem a bit strange at times. When I think about how out of place I feel in the city, I feel sorry for older folks who don't get into town that often.

I thought about this recently as I watched an elderly fellow try to get into a shopping mall. The old guy pulled on the door and nothing happened. So he pushed on it and this didn't work, either.

Soon the poor fellow was yanking and shoving on the door, and then just when he was sure the door was locked, it came unstuck and nearly knocked him down. He stumbled into the mall, mumbling to himself about these confounded new gadgets.

I was reminded of an old friend who accompanied me to a 4-H conference at a mid-western university. Jim had been a 4-H leader for many years but grew up during a time when people didn't travel like they do now. He had never been on an airplane, and although he was well past 70 years old, he probably hadn't been 100 miles from home in the past 40 years.

Jim may have been up in years, but he was ahead of his time really. He was practicing low-input agriculture before fertilizers and pesticides were invented and never got tangled up in the technological revolution. Plowing down some ryegrass and a little sheep manure was his idea of "pouring it on."

Jim was especially concerned about a healthful diet and swore he would never eat an apple if he couldn't find a worm in it. So we toured the university farms and looked at the test plots, all the while debating how a person could manage his soil so that the good micro-organisms would kick the stuffings out of the bad micro-organisms.

Then one evening Jim, my friend Mike, and I attended the big talent show in the coliseum. We got there a little early so we would have good seats, and Jim excused himself to go to the restroom.

I have been in those restrooms and remember that they were a little different than most. You entered through a door marked "Entrance" and then had to walk past the commodes and lavatories, and around a corner, to exit from a second door. The entrance door had no handles on the inside, so it was impossible to go out that way.

Mike and I sat in the coliseum for 20 or 25 minutes before we began to wonder what was keeping Jim. The restroom was just down the corridor and he couldn't have become lost in that distance.

Pretty soon the show began and still there was no sign of our old friend. By this time we were starting to worry; do you suppose we should go look for him?

About this time Jim comes walking down the aisle and I could see he was upset. He sat down beside me and I asked, "Where have you been? We were starting to worry about you."

"I've been in the *&#$ &*&#% restroom!" he said. "Somebody took the handles off the door, and I couldn't get the thing off the hinges. I had to wait for someone to come in and let me out!"

Death By Vitamin C

The science of nutrition has taken a beating recently. Just when everyone is convinced coffee gives a person headaches, a new study proves that coffee won't hurt you, but the person who brewed it might.

The newspapers and people like me should take part of the blame for this nutritional confusion. Every time someone comes out with a study, the papers report it as if it's the gospel truth.

Then when the whole thing is proven false, people like me repeat the story and try to make people laugh about it. Everybody knows nutritionists are just like kids: If you laugh at them, they act a fool more than ever.

I ran into a good one at a meeting recently. This fellow has just written a book on nutrition for dogs, and we were talking about some of his research.

How vitamin C got into the conversation is beyond me, but the author said flatly, "Dogs can't have vitamin C. Vitamin C will kill your dog. It destroys their liver and kidneys."

Just as I was about to ask how much vitamin C we were talking about, the conversation turned suddenly to the need for different foods for various breeds of dogs. This all makes sense when you think about it.

Everyone knows you can't feed a chihuahua the same thing you'd give a Labrador retriever. The Lab can easily eat a chicken, for example, whereas a meal like this could kill a chihuahua. You'd have to kill the chicken before you fed it to a chihuahua.

Then I realized this fellow had a point about vitamin C, too. We lost several dogs to this when I was a kid on the farm. In those days we didn't know much about nutrition and never recognized what caused their deaths.

Old Brownie would be a good example. Brownie died when he was about 14. He ate an orange when he was a pup, and now when I look back on it, I can see it finally got him.

And there was Blackie. I always thought Blackie died because we couldn't come up with more creative names for our dogs; but now I can see it was probably vitamin C.

Blackie was a short dog and never ate much fruit, but he ate lots of chicken liver. There's quite a bit of vitamin C in chicken livers.

Even that wouldn't have been so bad if he only ate livers from chickens we had slaughtered; but Blackie got to the point where he was getting them for himself. Obviously he ate one too many.

Then there was Gus, probably my favorite dog. Gus was the only beagle I've seen who could outrun three teenage boys for half a mile across a corn field and still flush a pheasant 60 yards out.

But while Gus was fast, he wasn't very smart. He liked to chase the milk truck. One day his feet slipped and the silver beast got him.

"Vitamin C?" you ask? No question about it: Milk is an excellent source of vitamin C.

The Other Woman

There's something about raising sheep that has a lasting effect on a person. Maybe it's the constant "baa — baa" in the lambing sheds, or the smell of orphan lambs sleeping behind the stove. Whatever it is, once a person has raised sheep he can never again be certified as normal.

I noticed this years ago when I was a county agent in Ohio. The county where I worked had a few thousand sheep, 40 thousand beef cattle, and a supply of hogs that would stretch from Columbus to Omaha if they all walked to market at the same time.

Still the most active commodity organization in the county was the sheep growers. These folks would have a big annual meeting and invite the whole town to a lamb dinner.

If all the sheep in that county were slaughtered the same day, a Rabbi could bless the whole flock before lunch, but the people who raised them were surely an enthusiastic bunch. Even more surprising was the fact that many members of the sheep growers association didn't own any sheep. These folks had a few woolies years ago, but now they just like to attend the annual meeting and sample the mint jelly.

I was thinking about this recently when my wife and I attended a sheep growers convention. It may seem strange for a person who owns only one sheep to attend a growers convention, but I told you what raising these animals does to a person.

Besides, I knew there would be others at the convention who don't own any sheep at all, and this was sure to be a fun bunch of people.

The convention had scheduled a wine tasting before dinner, and while that wasn't my main reason for attending, we got there in plenty of time. That's when I noticed there was something different here. Instead of tasting the wine, most folks just sat down to eat dinner.

I don't know if I've ever seen that before. The groups I normally associate with wouldn't think of eating before the wine was gone.

While this seemed strange enough, the legislative auction held after dinner was even crazier. The same people who passed up the wine tasting earlier bought bottles of wine from the auction like they were going out of style.

A bale of hay went for $280. A twisted bundle of baling wire brought 20 or 30 bucks. Nobody could tell what the bundle of wire was supposed to represent, but anyone who raises sheep knows wire is what holds everything together.

The most interesting item was a painting entitled "The Other Woman." If an artist had done "the lady that's known as Lou" from Robert Service's poem, "The Shooting of Dan McGrew," this would be the painting.

The auctioneer claimed this masterpiece would keep evil spirits out of the lambing barn, but the man who paid nearly $40 for it wasn't fooled. He took one look at "The Other Woman's" ghastly stare; then he donated the canvas back to the auction and kept the frame.

Mother Did It With Gravy

My television reported recently that today's teenagers are worried about their future. The news report said a survey asked high school seniors if they expected their lives to be better than the lives of their parents. Forty-seven percent of these teenagers said, "No".

Authors of the survey claim this shows how bad the economy has become. These people say young people should expect to eclipse their parents' standard of living. Each generation should have the ability to spend more money than the last.

That depends upon one's perspective, I guess. Maybe it's a good sign if teenagers don't expect to have more things than their parents. They might spend more time with their children and get off the merry-go-round society has built for itself.

My generation has more money than our parents ever thought about, but I don't think we are any happier. Nobody wants to return to the good old days, but there's something to be said for learning to do without — just in case you ever have to.

All of this came to mind recently when my wife and I went

out for dinner. We don't go out each month like the marriage counselors suggest a couple should. We skip a lot of months between dinners out. When we do go, I write about it in my column so I'll have a record that we went.

Dinner at the restaurant reminded me of the meals my mother used to fix. Restaurant meals are nothing like we had at home; but dinner out always reminds me that Mother fed her family for a month on what two meals cost us at the restaurant.

Others of my generation will remember how she did it, too. Mother did it with gravy. She could make gravy out of anything, and once we had gravy we almost always had something to put it on.

We put gravy on bread, toast, potatoes, rice, vegetables; and when times were tough, we put gravy on gravy. Can you imagine how many meals a person can make with $40 worth of gravy?

Mother had to have meat to make the gravy, of course, but we always had meat. My third grade teacher explained it this way, "You farm kids never have to worry about food. If you run out of money and need food, you can always go out and kill a pig."

We never killed a pig just to make gravy, but I suppose we could have. Mother made gravy from small bits of meat — ham, steak, chicken, rabbit, hamburger, even bologna. Some readers may balk at bologna gravy, but it's good if you're hungry.

Another economical dish my Mother used to make is "corn starch". Corn starch is made by mixing and heating milk, sugar, and of course, corn starch. It makes a hot, creamy breakfast to be served with toast on the side.

Corn starch may be short on fiber and it certainly wasn't invented by a nutritionist, but it had several things going for it. Corn starch was hot, it tasted good — and best of all, it was made by your mother. Research has proven the latter is still more important than all of the nutrients money can buy.

Evolution Explained

I get a kick out of newspaper stories about scientific theories, especially those relating to evolution and extinction of species. As we study the natural world a person can't help but marvel at the adaptations animals make for their protection and entertainment.

A recent news report says Florida has been invaded by the armadillo. The story describes the armadillo as "a primitive mammal looking like a cross between a turtle and a piglet."

To me, the armadillo looks more like a rat terrier shoved through a pineapple, but that's not the point of this story.

Florida scientists have learned the armadillo is poorly adapted to areas with highways. It collides with cars because of an earlier adaptation which causes this creature to jump as a response to fear.

Whereas an opossum faints when frightened, the armadillo leaps vertically into the air and lands on the road like a pineapple falling from a wagon. The jumping reflex that served the animal well when chased by hungry aborigines is no good at all when crossing highways.

While the unconscious highway possum has only a few tires to worry about, a freaked-out armadillo puts itself grill-high on a speeding Subaru.

We can see similar adaptations in our domestic animals. Cats are a good example. There was a time when cats lived in the barn and supported themselves by hunting mice and other small rodents.

Then our feline friends developed the habit of coming into the milking barn and whining for a squirt of milk. The fun-loving fellows doing the milking would then aim a part of the cow toward the cat and hose him down with milk.

That was fine when most farms milked a few cows, before we got milking machines, and parlors, and pipelines. Then by the time technology had eliminated the opportunity to squirt the cats, the beasts had long since lost their hunting instinct.

We still have the cat, however — an animal evolved from an earlier period, which spends most of its time sitting around whining for something to eat. Generations of cats fed from pans and saucers have become the modern day kitty with hardly enough guts to string a banjo.

The sheep is another example of domestic adaptations. It's hard to believe the sheep was once suited to the rough and rocky mountains of the world.

Through modern management and breeding this critter has degenerated into a weak and sniveling puffball. (Through no fault of the sheep farmer who remains a tough and hardy breed.)

The demise of the sheep was caused by economists, who continue to say the sheep should give birth in January to take advantage of spring lamb prices. This ill-planned birthing period has given us sheep that won't have lambs unless we put them in the barn and sit up all night boiling water.

Whatever happened to the tough and hardy woolies of the mountains? The coyotes got 'em, that's what! Between the coyotes and the economists a sheep hardly has a chance these days.

Baja, The Laughing Sheep

We won again! How can one family be so lucky as to win $2 million dollars and 5,000 square feet in Baja California, all in the same week?

That's what the contest mailers say: "Dear R. Pond, You are the winner! To claim your prize, you need only fill out the enclosed form and return it before common sense tells you this is a hoax."

I don't know why we are so lucky as to win all of these contests. Several years ago my son talked me into checking out one of these deals. The mailer said we had won a boat and motor. All we had to do was call the number listed in the mailer and they would tell us how to pick up our prize.

When I called, the man told me all we had to do was send them $200 for shipping and $350 for masking-tape on the package, and they would send the boat right out to us. I told him I really couldn't use that much tape, and a plastic boat shouldn't be all that hard to ship. We finally agreed he should keep the boat for use in his own bathtub.

But the latest prize was more appealing. Our own resort property in Baja. The photos show golf courses, tennis courts, young women.

My son says there's good fishing in that part of the world. I told him that "Baja" is Spanish for "laughing sheep," and that's the last thing I want to visit!

But he filled out the form and made me sign it. Then a few hours after the contest form was mailed, Russell and his mother informed me they had read the mailer a bit further to where it says the winner pays $39 per year for maintenance and upkeep on his Baja property.

My wife claims I come apart at times like this, but I don't really. If a person came apart, there would be lots of blood, some body parts, and other debris — not just frothy, blue smoke and thin streaks of bad language.

When something like this happens, I merely begin expressing opinions — blunt and controversial opinions. This time I said some bad things about Baja California, and about contests in general. I may have called Ed McMahon a crook. I can't remember.

There was talk about previous contests and the futility of mailing things off in the hope of receiving a 10-month cruise in North Dakota or a genuine Batman ring. I was especially critical of people who make me sign things without reading them.

My son says Baja sounds like a nice place, and he would like to go down and visit the property — do a little fishing, play some golf. He claims things around home are getting a bit dull, anyway.

I told him he could go places like that when he gets a few years older; and on his way home, maybe he could stop in San Diego and pick up that boat and motor we won two years ago!

Champagne Breakfast

I guess there are some things I'll never get used to. Things like mink coats, tuxedos, fluffy little dogs. Maybe I'm culturally impaired, I don't know.

Anything that seems a little bit extravagant makes me nervous. That's the way I felt recently when my wife and I accompanied friends for our first champagne brunch.

There's something about champagne for breakfast that's hard for me to get used to. I always associate champagne with celebrations and I hope for several more years before I start celebrating getting out of bed.

Then there's this "brunch" thing. Anyone who is used to three meals a day can see there's something shifty about a meal called brunch.

Where I grew up we had breakfast, dinner, and supper. If anyone tried to slip in a "brinner" or a "dupper" they were in for a heap of ribbing. Even the term "lunch" was considered a product of the city in those days.

But this champagne brunch was one of those buffet affairs

where you pay your money and then go back through the line as often as you wish. It's like you bet your stomach against the restaurant's cash register. You're calling their bluff in the hope you can eat more than they could possibly charge you.

And this buffet was a doozy. There was sausage, scrambled eggs, hashbrown potatoes, ham, bacon, seafood casseroles, ham with eggs on English muffins, waffles, cherry cobbler, blintzes, croissants, sweet rolls, and a complete array of salads and desserts.

Now you tell me, how is a person supposed to eat a breakfast like that? I never stand a chance at a buffet. Whenever I see a meal with more than three dishes, I freeze up.

There were seven kids in my family and three utensils of food was about all that could fit on the stove at one time; and I'll guarantee we all ate at one time. It wasn't like today when kids eat when they feel like it. A kid who missed meals in those days would be called Slim for the rest of his life.

We normally had meat and potatoes, and the third item was dessert. Dessert might be jello or peaches or green beans, but if it wasn't meat and potatoes it was dessert.

This caused some embarrassment the first time I went to eat with my wife's family. Connie's folks were town people and they were accustomed to having three or four vegetables with a meal.

I wasn't used to taking a little bit of this and a little bit of that; so when the mashed potatoes came around I took a bit less than I normally would.

Connie's younger sister shouted, "Hey, look! Roger took all the potatoes." She lied: I only took half of them.

Go Ahead And Threaten Them

We were just leaving the car and starting up the trail when we ran into this middle-aged sort of fellow, carrying a coffee can. "Boy, they sure are scattered this year. It's a funny year. There just aren't any berries. I've picked all morning and only got a couple of quarts," he said.

"Have you hiked back any further?" I asked.

"I've been all over. There just aren't any berries. It's a funny year," he repeated.

This man looked familiar. He could be the guy one sees peering from a truck window during deer season.

His story was the same, too. Change the word "berries" to "deer" and you have the deer hunter's story: "It's a funny year. No deer around here. I've been all over."

I started up the trail with wife and kids following. The kids were saying, "Why do we have to pick berries? The man said the berries are all dried up. Why do you always make us come up here and pick berries?"

"I'm taking you out in the woods to get you lost," I told

them, "And don't bother with the bread crumb trick. There are 30-pound chipmunks out here who just love bread crumbs."

"If you don't quit pestering me, I'll make you go down by the road to pick berries with that other guy," I added.

The psychologists say a person shouldn't threaten his kids, but I just can't help it during berry season. Besides, anytime a psychologist gives advice on raising kids, I say, "Let me see your kids."

I thought about the man near the road, and wondered if his father had threatened him as a child. He might have gotten further from his car if someone had scared him a little. I wondered who had forced him to go up into the mountains this particular day.

We used to pick blackberries when I was a boy, but I can't remember who made us do it. All I remember about picking blackberries is that the blue on your hands is berry juice, and the red on your arms is blood.

Huckleberry bushes don't have stickers like blackberry vines do. But those little, blue berries can cause your eyes to cross after awhile.

Notice I didn't say huckleberries are blueberries. They are little, blue berries; but calling a huckleberry a blueberry is like calling a grouse a chicken. People have been chased from the woods for less.

Many of the berry pickers I see nowadays are retired people, who have the time to go out and pick. These people appreciate wild berries. They grew up in the days when eating store-bought jelly was evidence of an unstable marriage.

But now most of the population just goes to the store and buys whatever they plan to eat for the next meal or two. If the markets closed, this country would starve to death before we figured out where food comes from.

Pup Tents

Now that the camping season is nearly over, I may have to break down and buy a tent. We have an A-wall tent, an umbrella tent, and a small cabin tent already; but each is too old, too large, or too embarrassing to set up in a civilized campground.

Besides, I get a kick out of looking at tents in the catalogs. The catalog shows a little, 7 X 8 foot structure and calls it a "three-man tent" or a "family tent." I don't know who tests these things, but it must be a family of Munchkins.

I had a tent like that when I was a kid. It cost $20 at the army surplus store.

A 7 X 8 structure was called a pup tent in those days, and these little tents were well-named. They were just the right size for a pup, but much too small for a full grown dog.

Mine was called a Mountain Pup Tent. The term "mountain tent" had a certain appeal for my 12-year-old mind, and the clerk assured me these were larger than the flatland tents.

This little tent taught me the two axioms of camping: There's no such thing as a waterproof tent, and camping is always fun for a little while.

One of my catalogs contains a 10 X 14 "Australian Walkabout Tent" that reputedly sleeps nine. I suppose nine people could sleep in a tent like that, as long as no one happens to wake up.

The only way to sleep nine in a space like this is to knock them out and drag them into the tent, one at a time.

After years of tenting experience I have concluded that designations like "four-man tent" or "family tent" has nothing to do with how many people the structure will house. These descriptions tell how many it takes to put the thing up.

My wife and I were talking recently with friends who have a 10 X 12 foot dome tent. This sounds like a good size for two adults and two kids. Unfortunately the tent takes four adults and three kids to set it up.

Our friends learned their tent will go up easily if they open a flap in one wall and hold onto the other side until the wind catches it just right. Then, the tent pops up and sits down like a hoop-skirt on a piano stool.

This technique works great when the wind isn't too strong. In a heavy wind the tent pops-up and takes the family to the next campground. Following a tent down the road while pretending your husband is a sky-diver is a lousy way to spend a vacation.

Each time I look at new tents I marvel at the construction. Everything is made of super-light materials and laced with screening for better air movement. Then you cover the tent with a rain-fly so you don't get wet.

I can't understand the need for all those screens. I don't sweat that much when I'm camping.

Maybe I don't need a new tent anyway. I'll just buy a little tarp for a rain-fly and cover the old cabin tent with it. That should cover up the mildew quite nicely.

Feeling His Oats

I've always enjoyed arguing with nutritionists. Not because I know anything about nutrition, but just because they are so much fun to argue with.

Anyone who wants a good argument these days can get one just by mentioning cholesterol. Within the past year I have read that lamb, beef, pork, buffalo, deer, elk, (and presumably porcupine) are lower in cholesterol and higher in protein than foods like chicken, turkey, salmon, and oatmeal cookies made with lard.

While all of these claims may seem conflicting, I think we can make sense out of them if we consider that saturated fat is a major culprit in the cholesterol problem. That's why a fat chicken is probably more dangerous than a lean steer from a dietary point of view.

I still believe all of these meats are good for people if we take it easy on the fat, and apply a little common sense to the issue. For example, I pride myself on harvesting a nice batch of low-cholesterol venison each year, but I'm always on the verge of a heart attack by the time I get it out of the field.

The best example of this loss of perspective is the wife who forced her husband to eat large amounts of oats to lower his cholesterol level. She took him to the doctor after several weeks and sure enough his cholesterol was way down.

This was O.K. until the old guy began eating oats three meals a day and actually seemed to develop a craving for this nutritious grain.

A few weeks later his face began to elongate. The wife had to cut his hair every few days to keep it from growing down his back in a luxurious mane.

He began jogging to lower his cholesterol still further, and then took up marathon racing. The wife finally realized what was happening when her husband began spending weekends at the race track.

First he just placed a couple of bets. Then, the old fellow began to jog around in the paddock area, and within a few weeks he was trotting around the track while the horses ran their warmups.

All of this time he ate more oats, until he was up to several pounds a day and could run like the wind, as they say in the movies. Finally, the wife knew she had to do something, so she called her brother, who trained horses and worked at a track in the East.

"I just don't know about Howard," she said. "He isn't interested in anything except oats and running, and he spends nearly all of his time at the track. It's getting to the point where I might as well be married to a horse," she sobbed.

"You shouldn't worry so much," her brother said. "Put a little molasses in his oats. Just give him his head, and he'll come around sooner or later."

"But it's so embarrassing," the wife said. "Like yesterday: Howard went down to the track and jogged around in the warmup area. Then one of those little jockey guys jumped on his back, and he ran around the entire track."

Her brother thought for a moment. Then he said, "Did you get a time on him?"

How To Discourage A Bird

No one enjoys seeing wildlife more than I do. The sight of a deer or a few pheasants can be the high point of the day, especially if a person's day is largely made up of low points.

My animal enthusiasm grows thin, however, when the wild critters start munching my green beans, or trying to remove insulation from the house. I can become very testy in those situations.

Some years ago a wild bird decided his reflection in our picture window was some type of enemy or an extremely good friend (only the bird knew for sure). This bird would begin crashing into the window about 5:00 each morning and kept it up until around lunch time.

The crashing and scratching was bad enough, but the mess on the window sill was nothing to sniff at, either. I was about to wish an unnatural death upon our feathered friend, when my wife's brother, Charlie, suggested we should discourage the bird with repellents.

Charlie had just finished a college degree in pest

management, and was eager to try the "old hawk scare" on the bonkers bird. We could make a silhouette of a hawk and hang it in the window.

I agreed to give it a try if Charlie would make the silhouette and hang it up. If the bird was still jumping at the window in two days, however, more severe means would be in order.

Two days later, Charlie was still reading about hawks and silhouettes, and the bird was still bashing his brains on my window. Once this bird was gone we haven't seen another Flatheaded Window-basher in the past 15 years.

I think this proves something, but I'm not sure what it is. Apparently reading about hawks is a good way to get rid of birds.

My wife had a similar experience with some deer recently. Connie became so enthused about flower gardening this spring that she created two huge flower beds and filled them with roses and colorful plants of all sorts.

The deer appreciated this so much they began walking through the beds, eating all they could and slobbering on the rest. Needless to say Connie began reading about deer repellents.

We learned that deer, unlike birds, don't care what you read about. So Connie tried the old trick of putting soap shavings in the flower beds to repel the deer.

The next day two deer walked through the beds — eating roses, washing their hooves, and blowing bubbles as they went.

This led to the human hair trick. Connie had her hair cut and brought all of the clippings home from the beauty parlor in a paper bag.

Unfortunately we left for vacation the next day and left the bag of hair sitting on the counter, instead of putting it in the flower beds. We returned to find the deer had not touched a thing all of the time we were gone, and didn't eat a single flower for more than a month.

The hair trick worked! The evidence is clear: Soap is not an effective deer repellent, but these beasts are scared to death of people with short hair.

Carpet Your Milk Can

Get more involved in the political process. Educate the public. Spend more for research and marketing.

These are familiar suggestions to anyone involved in farming or running an agricultural business. All this takes time and money, of course; and folks who have an excess of those two things aren't the ones who need better markets, more research, etc.

It seems when farm prices are at rock bottom everyone gets concerned about marketing; but that's the time when no one can afford to do anything about it.

That's how it was back in the '60s when my brother Jim attended a big commodity marketing meeting. The session was sponsored by a farm organization bent on doing something about the low price for milk and other agricultural commodities.

Meeting organizers pulled out all the stops. The auditorium was packed, there were talks by local and state organizers, and all of this was capped-off with a speech by the organization's national president.

You could see someone had put a lot of money into this shindig, but those in attendance didn't think much about it until the program was nearly over. Then they found out.

All of the expenses hadn't been paid yet. The plan was that everyone would be so enthused by the president's speech, the remaining expenses could be paid through donations.

It almost worked. The national president was terrific, and by the time he sat down the audience was ready to march.

Then one of the organizers stood up and said, "We really appreciate our president coming all of this way to speak to us tonight. If you will just drop your contribution in the milk can here in front, it will help pay part of his expenses. Your support is greatly appreciated."

That's when Jim knew he was in trouble. He was sitting right next to the milk can and would be one of the first to leave the auditorium. And all he had in his pocket was a $20 bill and a penny!

With the price of milk the way it had been, $20 was a lot of money. Maybe a week's salary. A penny on the other hand is a tough way to begin a collection.

And a milk can! Anyone who has ever dropped a penny in a milk can will attest that it's noisy.

First there's a clang from the coin's initial impact, followed by several bounces, and then the one-cent piece runs around the can until it loses steam, finally settling down with the faint tinkle of a tiny doorbell. An entire auditorium can almost hear the whiskers on Honest Abe's face as they brush against the can.

I never learned how the rest of the donations turned out that evening. Jim says he never looked back to find out. One of his friends still reminds him of the occasion, but there's no reason to feel bad about it.

Anyone who solicits money from farmers when prices are down had better take the time to put some carpet in his milk can.

Time To Think

I have always thought farmers are the world's smartest people. Few professions require more ingenuity and daily decision-making than farming. If you talk to real commercial farmers, you will find as a group they are very intelligent people.

But making decisions isn't what makes these folks so smart in my opinion. I think farmers develop their intelligence by driving tractors. A person who is out on a tractor for 10 hours a day has almost unlimited thinking time.

Several years ago an old friend told me his dad used to warn, "Never try to outsmart a farmer. They spend so much time driving a tractor, with nothing to do but think; they will get the best of you every time."

This thought came to mind this morning as I was staring at my computer screen and trying to think of something to write. "This is just like driving a tractor," I thought. "The main difference is I don't know where I'm going."

Actually the difference is not all that great. I drove tractors as a kid and often didn't know where I was going then, either.

The biggest problem with driving a tractor is the tendency for a person's thinking to dissolve into daydreaming. Sometimes a guy gets to ruminating so much, he forgets what he's supposed to be doing.

You can get by with a certain amount of daydreaming when disking or working plowed ground, but there's nothing more embarrassing than making a lap around the field and finding the machinery came unhooked on the previous round.

My brother used to laugh at me for not looking back to see what was happening behind; but I will always remember the day he drove all the way around the field without any wire in the baler. Those little square chunks of hay were real obvious when he came around on the next windrow.

I have always thought writing is a lot like driving tractors. There is plenty of time to think when you are writing; and like the farmer a writer can't always tell when his implements aren't working. I have written entire stories only to realize later they made no sense whatsoever.

For me writing is like entering a newly plowed field — rough and full of clods; then, working it over and over until you get so disgusted you go ahead and plant it anyway. Who knows if it's any good?

There's no question that writers and farmers have a lot in common. Like farmers, writers are constantly thinking, and folks who use their brains that much are almost sure to develop some intelligence sooner or later.

This whole idea made sense to me when I first thought about it, but now that I've mulled it around all morning one thought keeps coming back. "If writers and farmers are so darned smart, then why don't we make any money?"

Newfangled Gadgets

I've never been much of a shopper. If I had a choice between going shopping and having a tooth pulled, I would probably go shopping, but I still wouldn't like it.

Looking for a new car is about the worst kind of shopping in my opinion. The high price tag for cars is part of the problem, but the traditional dickering about price is a hassle, too.

I've always hated those deals where the salesman won't tell you the price of a car. You have to make him an offer; then he checks with the boss, and they both have a big laugh before he returns to tell you how much everyone enjoyed your little joke.

Many car dealers are beginning to realize customers don't like all of this hokus pokus about prices. When we bought a car recently the salesman said, "Our dealership thinks buying a car should be just like buying a pair of shoes. We tell you what the price is and if you like the product, and the color, you can decide if this is what you want."

"That's certainly good to hear," I told him. "That's the way I like to do business."

So the salesman told me how much they needed for the car, and I offered him $1,000 less. Maybe I was just testing him, I don't know.

We bought the car, anyway, and it happens to be a Honda. I know folks will object to buying foreign cars and all of that; but I figure anything made at Marysville, Ohio isn't all that foreign.

I was talking recently with a woman who says she and her husband bought a new Buick to help support the American car makers. They later noticed the interior of their Buick is exactly like the inside of a new Toyota.

If you watch cars going down the road, you'll notice the outsides are all the same, too. Some coincidence, huh?

The biggest surprises for me are the safety gadgets in cars these days. There's a bell to remind that the door is open, a beeper to make you fasten the seatbelt, and a buzzer to indicate your leg is caught in the steering-wheel.

Our Honda even has an automatic seatbelt. One end of the belt runs on a little track above the door frame. When you turn the key on, the seatbelt zips up the track and holds you in. Then, when you open the door, the belt zips back and lets you out.

If you are backing the car and open the door to stick your head out, the seatbelt grabs you by the neck and throws you in the sideditch. This teaches one to use the mirrors.

It seems we have come full-circle when it comes to vehicle safety. The philosophy behind these new gadgets is just like the old buggy horses my Dad used to drive.

The old horses and these new cars have the same code of safety: If you do something foolish, they make you pay for it.

Throwing Them Back
(In The Bushes)

It just didn't seem right. Here we were stumbling along the bank, braving wind and rain to catch a fish that isn't fit to eat.

Shad fishing: Next to golfing that must be about the biggest waste of time anyone could come up with. But my son wanted to go, and of course I enjoy catching fish, too (even if they are full of bones).

There's no better expression of the generation gap than the way people respond to sport fishing. It wasn't that long ago when folks who fished for things they couldn't eat were considered a bit weird at best.

I remember the time my wife, Connie, and I took my parents fishing in Quebec. Dad never had time for such things when he was farming, and Mother hadn't been fishing since she was five years old.

We were on the Ottawa River, where bass and walleye rub fins in the narrows and northern pike cruise the backwaters. The river was high and the action so slow for the first couple of days that we were wondering if we had come to the right place.

123

That's when I learned that Mother and Dad saw fishing as something more than a sport. They wanted to catch something — and they planned to eat what they caught!

Connie and I arrived back at the cabin after the second day of fishing to find Dad cleaning up some chubs for dinner. He pretended not to know these were chubs, but I think he just couldn't stand to waste all that time without catching something to eat. We tried them, and they were awful.

But, the third day we got into 'em: Bass and catfish in sizes and numbers to eliminate any chance of starvation and make overeating a real possibility. The fourth day we nailed them, again. We caught bass so fast you could hardly take one off your hook fast enough to get back to fishing.

That's when I learned Dad had left his bifocals at the cabin and couldn't see to tie on hooks. Each time he broke off a hook I was tying a new rig for him. I also learned Connie liked to fish, but had never taken a fish off the hook. So each time she caught one, I was unhooking it for her.

All this time my line was in the boat! The bass were biting like crazy, and I was stringing fish and trying to thread a line through those tiny, little eye's one finds in a number 6 baithook.

When the next fish came in, I told Connie, "Sorry, I'm going to fish. You're gonna have to take that one off yourself." She refused — for about 30 seconds — and then she learned how easy it is to unhook fish.

About this time I learned Dad isn't real keen on the idea of releasing fish. Once he catches them he figures they're his, and nothing short of the mounted police is going to get them back in the water.

I finally got him to put the small ones back and then sorted the live ones out of a bucket to stay under our limits. We had just the right number of fish on the stringer, but when we arrived at the cabin I began finding extras. Either Dad had another bucket in the boat somewhere — or he was hiding them under his shirt!

Looking Back

There's that old feeling again. It's the late innings, your elbow hurts, and the pain in your glove hand confirms your worst fears: The catcher is firing the ball to the mound harder than you are throwing it to the plate.

That's the way I felt this week when I read a letter from a fellow in the Midwest. Here I am making a living (of sorts) telling stories, and this guy has stories better than anything I've thought up in months.

The fellow says my column about driving tractors and forgetting the machinery reminds him of two hired men he worked with years ago. Both of these fellows stayed out late at night and had trouble staying awake during the day.

One day the letter-writer came across one fellow standing in front of a tractor with a disk on behind. He was pulling at something under the front wheels of the tractor.

When my correspondent got closer, he asked the man what was wrong and the fellow looked up in anger. "Some stupid *&#$*@ left a harrow out here in the field!" he yelled.

The man was so mad his face was red as a beet, and scarcely changed hues when he learned the harrow was the one he had been pulling behind the disc. The harrow had come unhooked the previous round, and the fellow had driven the front wheels right up in the middle of it.

The letter writer also recalls the days when growing up on a dairy farm often produced a sincere and uncompromising hatred of cows. He and his brothers milked by hand, each waiting eagerly for the day they turned 18, when they could enlist in the army and escape the cows.

Because their father was a salesman and away from home much of the time, the boys would slip off to town and sign up for the draft before Dad could put a stop to their unbridled patriotism. One older brother ran into a snag, however. The week he turned 18, he packed a bag and decided to hitchhike the 20 miles to the county seat to sign up for the draft.

As soon as the morning milking was completed, he cleaned-up and walked to the road and stuck out his thumb. The first two cars passed him by, but the third stopped, and he got in.

It was Dad! He had returned from a trip two days early, and had one good question: "Where do think you're going in the middle of the day, when you ought to be out in the field cultivating corn?"

The letter writer was more fortunate and managed to get into the army without hitching the wrong ride. He remembers his first night at Fort Gordon, Georgia, and his fear that any place of that size must have some cows around somewhere.

The writer had never been out of Ohio before joining the army, and in those days his vision of Hell was a great, big farm with a whole bunch of dairy cows. He was sure some big-mouthed sergeant was going to make him milk cows twice a day.

To make a long story short, this fellow and his letter saved my life that day. I had two columns due and was up against the deadline.

Some people might say I should send him my week's salary for sending me these stories. I wouldn't go quite that far, but I did send him a free book. Some weeks that's about all the salary I get, anyway.

Our "Go To" Guy

I knew it would happen sooner or later. Government agencies have progressed to the point where they are so busy recycling paper that they don't have time to shuffle it. Agencies have become so concerned about recycling paper that they are sending out directives printed on, what else? Millions of tons of paper!

I was told that one agency sent a directive to all of the outlying offices to explain their new recycling program. This missive decrees that colored paper should no longer be used because it is less recyclable than white paper.

But what did they print it on? Blue paper! I wonder if anyone has considered how much paper folks could conserve by not writing reports on the stuff.

When I see something like this, I remember a county agents' meeting back in the '60s. The federal extension service came up with a new reporting program, and each state had meetings to tell county agents how to keep track of their time.

I was working in Ohio, and we all went to Dayton for three

days of meetings. The alleged purpose of this new program was to make reporting easier, but everyone knew there was a rat in the woodpile.

For two days the meeting organizers skirted the issue. Then just before adjournment on the third day, the big boys dropped the bomb.

"If you will just look at these new report forms, you can see they allow you to record how much time is spent on each activity. It's not necessary to record these things by minutes, but half-hour time blocks are certainly appropriate."

We couldn't believe it. Some days a county agent can hardly remember all that he did, let alone record it in half-hour blocks. He would have to take a second person along to keep the records.

They said Congress needed this information. Most of us figured Congress needed this stuff like they needed another hole in the head.

Then, my old friend Maynard stood up to clear the air. Maynard was the county agent at Chillicothe, Ohio, and he could put things into perspective better than anyone I've ever known.

He was what the basketball coaches would call our "go to guy." We counted on him to keep the meetings lively, and if anyone should be told where to go, he was the guy to do it.

"Well, I think this is just wonderful," he told the group. "You are probably aware that Chillicothe is home to the Mead Paper Company and is the white paper capital of the world. I figure this new reporting program should just about double the demand for paper in this part of the country. Mead will probably have to build on to their mill!"

I left Ohio many years ago, and I'm told that Maynard has since retired. I suspect he got out just in time. I wouldn't want to be around when someone tried to make him sort his waste paper into three separate boxes.

Antiques

"What's that?" the boy asked, as a hunk of metal clanged across the counter and fell to the floor.

"Oh, just something falling off the wall," I replied. "Here it is, a corn dryer, and here's the corn. Looks pretty dry to me.

"This is an antique. See, it's a piece of iron which allows you to impale six ears of corn and hang them in your kitchen to dry. The pioneers used to dry whole corn fields this way — before we had corn cribs or propane and batch dryers," I explained.

My son had lost interest. Once the fallen object was identified, that's all he wanted to know. Isn't that typical of young people? Absolutely no appreciation for antiques.

The boy may have detected a note of sarcasm. That's another thing about young people: They don't understand good sarcasm.

This wasn't the first time I had looked at the corn dryer and wondered why the pioneers would hang six ears of corn in their kitchen. As I picked it off the counter this time, I thought, "Some guy in Vermont is sitting in his workshop right now and chuckling to himself as he turns out these brand new antiques by the gross."

Then I looked at the rows of old stuff lining the kitchen walls and creeping across the shelves — built for holding these things. The Revere lantern was the first to catch my eye. Now there's an item deserving further study.

The Revere lantern resembles nothing more than the roof vent from a fancy out-house. It's about four inches in diameter and made of pierced tin — the kind you would use in the front of a pie safe (which is another subject).

A Revere lantern looks like someone cut about a foot off one of those little, round roof vents — the ones with the Chinese hats on top. Then, he set it on the fence and used it to check the pattern of his 16-gauge.

Then, the craftsman walks around to the other side and fires the second barrel. He solders a tin bottom on it, cuts a door in the front to allow placing a candle in the thing; and he's got a brand new, antique Revere lantern.

When a person puts a candle in one of these and lights it, he can see the holes in the side. Otherwise, he can't see a thing he couldn't see without the lantern.

I used to think the Revere lantern was a replica of the one Paul carried on his famous ride. A closer look, however, would suggest it probably wasn't.

How would you like to go riding around the countryside, balancing a candle in a tin can and shouting insults at the British army? Although I would admit this lantern looks like it has insulted somebody.

Can you imagine Paul riding into town with his reins in one hand and one of these tin candle-holders swinging from the other, and shouting, "The British are coming! The British are coming!"

People would say, "We can see they're coming, Paul; They've already shot the devil out of your lantern!"

"Here Kitty"

The world would be a better place if each household had a cat — and nobody had more than one. Excess cats can be a burden, but a country place needs at least one to keep the rodents in line.

Cats are always an experience at our house. Maybe it's just bad luck, but we've found that a cat needs a full complement of nine lives if he's going to survive around here.

We recently picked up a new kitten from friends who live on a farm. Our friends had two to choose from. One was small and gentle, and the other was larger — but a bit wild.

I talked my wife into taking the wild one because I want a cat that can stand up for himself — one that strikes fear into the hearts of small mammals. A cat that can hunt bulldogs with a switch.

We put the kitten in the bathroom the first night so he wouldn't run off. When my wife left for school the next morning, I promised to put the kitty in the shop. I had carried the kitten only a few yards when I thought, "This cat isn't so wild. He would stay around if I just put him down near the house."

The kitten's feet had barely hit the ground when he took off as if he planned to run the thirty miles back to his old farmstead. I couldn't catch him, but finally headed him off and chased him nearer the house. Then, I remembered the dog. "If I let the dog out of his pen, he will run around the house, and the kitten will run up a tree."

It worked! The cat went up an oak tree, and I had him under control. (If 30 feet from the ground in the top of an oak tree is "under control.")

Whoever said, "What goes up must come down" has never seen a cat in a tree. The cat finds going up so much easier than coming down, he just keeps going until he runs out of tree; then he whines until someone gets him down.

A city resident might call the fire department in a situation like this, but you can't do that in the country. If I call the Rural 7 Volunteers to get my cat out of a tree, I might as well dial the moving company and have them start packing our furniture. A person just doesn't live something like that down.

So I waited until my son, Russell, got home from school. Then I got out the old extension ladder and went up to have a chat with the kitty. By this time the cat was 30 feet from the ground and still climbing.

I had already determined I couldn't climb down the ladder with a cat scratching me from elbow to elbow. So we rigged up a 10 by 20-foot sheet of plastic as a safety net. (For the cat. I prefer to work without a net.)

We tied the plastic to four trees so it hung about 3 feet off the ground. When the cat hit the plastic Russ was supposed to catch him in a salmon dip net to prevent another runaway.

I reached up toward the cat. "Nice kitty. That's a nice kitty. Just stick your leg over here, and we'll be out of this tree in no time."

Then, "Awrrr, Phfft!, Phfft!, Arawrwrrrrr! Yeoww-r-r-r-r! Ker-thump!"

"Get the net! Get the net!"

Whoomp! "Got him!"

"Good job, Russ! Now, put the cat in the shop; and call the fire department to see if they can get me out of this tree."

Experts Won't Let You Watch

I guess I will never be an expert. An expert needs a certain personality — a confident air, the nerve to pretend he knows things he really isn't too sure about.

I've tried it a couple of times, but I always give myself away by telling folks how much I don't know. Even worse, I demonstrate my ignorance right before their eyes.

This happened again recently when my friend, Bud, asked if he could come over and watch me cut-up a deer. Bud has never hunted deer but thought watching me cut venison might contribute to his knowledge of the sport.

I said, "Sure, come on over. I might not be the best meat cutter in the world, but you're welcome to watch."

That's the same thing I said when Terrence asked to watch me shear sheep several years ago. "Sure, I'm probably the world's worst sheep shearer, but watching me might help you learn what not to do," I told him.

An expert would never say something like that. The expert would say, "Oh, I won't be shearing this week. I'm just getting packed for the National Sheep Shearers', Meat Cutters', and Fish Scalers' Convention down in Saragosa Springs."

Not me though, I tell them to come right ahead. Terrence watched me shear the sheep — and said, "I don't think those ewes look so bad. You got all the wool off them."

I have a shearing chart for the sheep and a cutting chart for deer, but this does little to boost my credibility. Some think I'm confusing the charts — cutting-up the sheep and shearing the deer. The similarities in my technique are frightening.

Terrence told an acquaintance, "Roger looked at the shearing chart to see where all of the cuts should be made. Then, he laid the chart aside and just went every-which-way."

I cut deer the same way. Bud arrived just as I located my extension service bulletin on how to bone-out a deer. I looked at the book briefly and laid it on a nearby table. Then, I picked up my knife and just went berserk.

I told Bud, "If I cut around the hind leg here, I can separate it from the pelvic bone or whatever this is. Then I can cut and pull these muscles apart.

"I cut most of this into round steaks. We like our steaks thick — but not quite as thick as this one."

"This muscle here might be the sirloin tip," I continued, "but that won't matter because it's going to be a roast, anyway."

After a few more cuts and considerable pulling, I had the leg cut into five pounds of steak, ten pounds of hamburger, and one small roast. "Our family really likes venison hamburger," I commented.

I've never claimed to be an expert at cutting meat, but I'm getting better. Once I get going, I can cut an entire deer in about three hours.

If you think that's slow, you should see me shear the sheep.

Road Hunters

I grew up reading outdoor magazines: Field & Stream, Sports Afield, Outdoor Life — those were the literary fodder of the day.

I'm not sure if it's me or the magazines, but something has changed over the years. It's true I no longer float the creek on the inverted hood from a Chrysler, or pack into the woods to hunt squirrels with my sling shot; but outdoor writers have changed, too.

The old-timers like Corey Ford, Ted Trueblood, and H.P. Davis (you can see how old I am) are gone; and with them went a lot of good stories and real outdoor experiences.

The articles I read now seem to be written by hardware salesmen and travel agents. If you can't buy it at your local supplier, they'll tell you how to get there by boat, plane, or air-conditioned camel.

Some of the most entertaining outdoor stories are about preparations for the big game seasons. Modern writers suggest everything from watching TV with your eyes closed (improved hearing) to jogging to the bathroom (avoiding embarrassment in the campgrounds) as good exercises for hunting season.

A recent article recommends that elk hunters arrive in camp several days early so they will have time to become acclimated before the hunt. The writer assumes these hunters are city dwellers with a tendency to wheeze when breathing unleaded air.

Surely the author knows arriving several days early is an old tradition for elk hunters. Many of these Nimrods head for camp several days before the season and are still playing cards a week after the whole thing is over.

I know hunters who arrive in camp years before they go hunting. Others haven't been in the woods since the time that young kid killed an elk and ruined the week for the entire camp.

I suppose we should recognize that deer hunters have similar tendencies, but are far less prone to faulty acclimatization. Some deer hunters stay in their vehicles throughout the season, allowing them to breathe the same old air they are accustomed to.

My son and I saw a hunter last year who was surely out of place in the woods. He drove an orange Mazda sedan with a four speed transmission — and cruised the forest in a perfect imitation of a hummingbird with a road map.

It was bow season for elk, and we hunted an area where there are a lot of roads. Each time we walked out of the forest, there was an awful humming sound and this fellow would go buzzing past like a blazing, orange hornet. He could do 30 miles an hour on the curves and nearly 50 on the straight-aways.

We tried to analyze his hunting technique, but couldn't figure him out. Robin Hood himself couldn't have stopped that Mazda and shot at an elk with his bow.

The only conclusion we could draw was that this guy had mounted a broadhead on his hood ornament and planned to puncture an elk before it could stop laughing and jump off the roadway.

Pony Sign

One of the privileges of farming and other types of self-employment is the opportunity for a family to work together. The concept of husband and wife, mother and daughter, father and son, toiling side-by-side is part of the American ideal.

It's no bed of roses, however. Family members don't react like other employees, and when spouses share business decisions one little disagreement can lead to six weeks on the hide-a-bed.

That's the way it is at my house, anyway. My wife and I try to make business decisions together, but our philosophies are not always in sync.

My wife and I come from two schools of economic thought. Whereas I belong to The Royal Order of Skeptics, Connie has an M.B.A. from the Massachusetts Institute of Blind Faith.

Her business philosophy says, "If you work hard and do a good job, the money will be there." I tell her that is the belief of poor people around the world.

When Connie finds a check in the mail she thinks of all the bills it will pay. I look at the check and wonder what the bank

137

will charge us to deposit it.

A person can attend family business seminars and counseling services to mitigate problems such as these, but there's only so much you can do with a person's innate tendencies. I've tried to overcome my pessimism, but I know there's no use.

I think the best way to understand conflicting business philosophies is to recall the story of two young boys at Christmas. One little boy was such a pessimist that his parents always went out of their way to make him happy. His brother, on the other hand was so optimistic that the parents worried he might not survive in the real world.

So one Christmas Mom and Dad decided to give the boys widely divergent presents in an attempt to influence their personalities. For the little pessimist they got a fancy electric train, with remote control, model train-station, and a complete city surrounding the tracks.

Then, for the hopelessly optimistic youngster they got a handful of horse manure and wrapped it in a shoebox. Not your usual present to be sure, but the parents hoped to discourage the little optimist long enough to get his attention.

When the boys opened their presents on Christmas Eve the pessimist looked at his nice new train set and began to cry something fearful. He said the train would probably jump the tracks the first time he played with it, and all that shiny paint was sure to chip and scratch at the slightest bump. Nothing his parents could say made him feel any better.

Then the optimistic youngster opened his little box of roadapples and just squealed with delight. He ran through the house, clapping his hands and shouting, "Oh boy! Oh boy! This is great! I just know there's a pony around here somewhere."

How To Burp A Cow

Where is the greenhouse effect when we need it? Last year the country's mid-section suffered one of the driest years ever, and crops baked through the summer.

The news media said it was the greenhouse effect. All of that pollution is heating up the earth, and it's only a matter of time until we will be plowing the cornbelt with camels.

This spring the eastern cornbelt was plagued with cool weather and floods. A man with an ark was reportedly bidding on livestock in Kentucky. Now I ask you, "Whatever happened to the greenhouse effect?"

Last fall I read that forest fires in California produced so much smoke a little town called "Happy Camp" was fogged-in for weeks, during which time the temperature dropped 20 degrees below normal. The scientist featured in the story says this gives credence to the nuclear winter theory: Too much smoke in the atmosphere shuts out the sun's rays, causing a cooling effect.

Now, the New York Times News Service reports German

scientists have learned that savanna fires in Africa are causing both global warming and acid rain. They say methane and carbon dioxide released from man-made fires may be contributing to the greenhouse effect.

A few months ago I read that a fellow in Colorado was studying the amount of gas given off by a cow. He concluded belching cows are a major contributor to global warming.

Yesterday, my wife read a letter to the editor in an urban newspaper in which a lady writes that South American farmers are burning primeval forests to create more grazing land. The letter-writer insinuated that folks who eat beef are contributing to this destruction.

At first glance these stories may seem unrelated, but the steady eye will see a pattern. Each is a tale of gloom perpetrated by someone who doesn't have anything more urgent to worry about. These people should have some kids or livestock to occupy their time.

Then, if we look closely we'll see these problems are actually solving themselves. According to the papers the greenhouse effect and nuclear winter theories offset each other. One theory causes some months to be cold, and the other causes particular months to be warm. Weather records will show these trends have already begun.

We can also see the cow-belching specialist and the lady who doesn't like beef have a few rocks in their blender. First, anyone who has been around cows will tell you being belched at isn't the worst thing that can happen.

Second, it's true South American farmers are creating more smoke and more cows. This may increase the gas load in the atmosphere.

On the other hand, studies have shown the more folks we have eating beef, the fewer we have eating beans. I rest my case.

Just Coasting

You can learn a lot about a person just by looking at his equipment. Some folks always boast a top-of-the-line outfit, while the rest of us seem to make do with whatever is handy. The people who have the good equipment would no sooner tie up a muffler with baling wire than go to church in their coveralls.

Years ago I hunted quail with a friend who always had nice equipment. John would get out of the car, uncase his little 20-gauge Beretta, and wonder if we might get into some briars where the gun's stock could be scratched.

I in turn would drag out my old Stevens-Fox, mutated years ago to resemble an English double (as much as it could anyway). The old Fox was a cheap gun from the beginning and twenty years of ownership afforded me the courage to attack it with a hacksaw, chopping off the pistol grip and sanding the bulky, beavertail forearm into something a little more petite.

Even though I keep threatening to buy a new shotgun, there's a certain amount of comfort in knowing I could drop this one off a cliff without shedding a tear. My shotgun handles O.K., but I wouldn't want to lay it down next to my friend's Beretta.

You can see similar contrasts by driving into any farmstead in the country. Some will have brand new equipment and fresh paint on the buildings, while others are still waiting for their ship to come in.

Anyone who drives into my place can see my ship is probably not coming: It's lost at sea.

Our place is not a farm, but merely a rural residence with just enough space for things that wouldn't look right in town. Things like an old Case tractor, some sheep, a bird dog and a few bales of hay.

The first thing a visitor sees is the orange tractor, parked just off the lane at the top of a hill. The second thing one notices is a roll of fence.

Anytime you see an old tractor with a roll of fence nearby you can be sure the owner would rather be fishing than plowing or fixing the corral.

I park my tractor at the top of the hill because it doesn't have a battery. The first time I read about the celebrated Nebraska Tractor Test I thought it was a trial to determine if the machine would start on the level. My tractor would never start in Nebraska.

I've always thought living on a hillside provides a certain measure of competence. When a vehicle's battery goes dead, you can coast the rig down the hill to start it. If the machine doesn't run by the time it reaches the bottom, there's not a whole lot more a person can do for it.

Just this week I noticed my son's motorbike was laying next to the lane at the bottom of the hill. That bike hasn't run for two years, but the boy keeps coasting it down toward the road trying to start it.

I'm afraid that will be the final test for this place. When you see all of our machinery at the bottom of the lane, you'll know we've gone out of business.

Don't Confuse The Animals

Everyone has his favorite signs of spring. For some it's the appearance of robins on the lawn, while others look for their friends returning from Hawaii.

My favorite sign of spring is a group of lambs romping around the pasture — someone else's pasture. It's not that I don't like sheep or anything like that, but we've had sheep just long enough to know how cute they can be in someone else's pasture.

I've learned that once the lambs finish romping through the field, the whole bunch will go traipsing through the yard and mow down the petunias.

As my kids have grown older our sheep have done likewise, and we are finally down to one ewe, the last survivor of a hardy band. I've reached the point where I can shear the whole flock in one day.

Most folks don't realize that one sheep is the ideal number for a small farm. One is so easy to keep track of, and anyone who can't keep that many together had better stay in the house.

Some people ask me, "How can you keep just one sheep? Doesn't it get lonely?"

"No," I tell them, "Sheep don't think about loneliness. The only reason sheep flock together is the wool in their eyes gives them terrible eyesight. The herding instinct has evolved to assure they will bump into something soft."

It's hard for humans to understand how animals feel about things. A good example of this is the orphan lamb a lady wrote to me about last winter.

When the letter writer was a little girl she had a pet lamb named "Jim" who was raised on a bottle. Jim was a great pet, but spent so much time around the house he didn't know he was a sheep.

One day a large band of sheep was driven by the ranch on the way home from pasture, and Jim was so frightened by all the bleating and blatting, he ran right through the screen door to get into the house.

Some years back my daughter had a similar experience with a pig that was nearly convinced he was a sheep. This pig was underweight for the county fair and had to be kept around for an extra month or so to qualify for the freezer.

We just put the pig out with the sheep and fed him a couple of times a day. There was no problem with the sheep eating the pig's feed; His mannerisms were just more than they could stomach.

But the pig ate with the sheep, and wandered around the pasture just as if he was part of the flock. The first few times the pig went out for pasture one could almost see the consternation on his face. "What in the world are you guys eating out here?" he seemed to ask.

I don't know if the pig was lonely or not, but there was never any question he would have deserted his friends and changed religions for a decent place to eat.

144

Changing Times

You can hardly turn around these days without seeing someone trying to look or feel younger.

This is O.K., I guess, but a good memory would remind many folks that being young is a lot harder than it looks. Times have changed, and I think the baby boom generation is more out-of-touch than many of us realize.

Kids today probably face more pressures than my generation confronted when we were growing up; but growing up wasn't easy in those days, either.

I think dating was and is the hardest part of adolescence. When I was a young man about the only place you could take a date was to the bowling alley or a movie.

It wasn't very long until you had seen every film on the market and a fellow's arm was completely out of joint. Then you had to go bowling.

Once a guy was old enough to drive, he could take a date to a drive-in movie; but that was before daylight savings time ruined the drive-in business. By the time it gets dark enough to

145

show an outdoor movie nowadays you could have been bowling for four hours.

Now everyone has a VCR at home and the kids can rent more movies than the cinema could show in an entire summer.

But I think the thing that totally revolutionized dating was the advent of bucket seats. Very few cars had bucket seats when I was a kid, and I'm sure the guys in Detroit didn't know what they were doing to society when they came up with the idea.

I believe bucket seats and the gear shift on the floor are the two major contributors to the marital instability we see in the U.S. today. How can young people develop a close and lasting relationship when they are constantly separated by a gearshift and a console?

The old Chevys and Fords we used to drive didn't require a whole bunch of gear shifting, either. You just put the car in "drive", and you drove.

Any boy who was old enough to date quickly learned to steer with one hand, and we figured anyone who couldn't drive several miles with one knee was not much of a driver.

Of course those were the days when double dating was about the only way young people went on dates. It was more of a practical matter than anything else: You didn't really need the extra company, but somebody had to drive.

With the old style seats kids got acquainted on the way to the movie and on the way back. There was never any of this shouting back and forth that seems prevalent among high school kids today.

I don't have any idea how young people go on dates these days. Sometimes I think back to my youth, and realize maybe I don't really want to know.

These Cameras Have Ears

I grew up in a time when people didn't have the things families now consider essential. Television was just becoming popular, nobody had a microwave oven, and Mothers recorded all of the important events with a Kodak Brownie camera.

Now we zap dinner in the microwave, set the VCR to record a favorite TV program, and hurry out to the ball park to video tape the kid's first home run. I've adjusted to most of this, but one thing I can't get used to are those new video cameras.

It seems there's no limit to what folks can do with those things. A guy can go into a store, plop down $1,000, and suddenly he's Cecil B. DeMille.

Pretty soon he's taping his wife having babies, the dog chasing cats, and the garbage truck running over his can. Before you know it there's more film in the closet than Gene Autry has in his museum.

Even though I don't own a video camera, I have watched enough tape to know there are three basic rules to video taping: Hold the camera still, don't let the kids see you coming, and don't forget these cameras have sound!

The first rule, holding the camera still, is important anytime you want to show videos to folks who don't respond well to motion sickness. My wife once watched a walking tour of her sister's house with such intensity that she was rendered pale green — not with envy, but motion sickness.

Connie watched the paintings jiggle and walls go by until she was obliged to crawl from the room and hold onto the floor until her eyeballs quit scrolling up and down.

The second rule, don't let them see you coming, applies to families with small children. Once the kids get used to being filmed, they begin to play to the camera.

My four-year-old niece, for example, saves her best act and most embarrassing dialogue for those times her Mom is taping the action. If home videos were rated, she'd be PG-13.

This leads to the third rule, don't forget these machines have sound. A friend spent two weeks on a fishing boat in Alaska, where he filmed miles of unidentified scenery and hundreds of generic fish. He was back home before he realized the only sound on the video tape is, "I think I got one."

Another friend, his wife, and their high-school-age sons also traveled to Alaska and filmed the catching of dozens of salmon; but they did a better job of adding sound to their videos.

One day it seemed the father had just the right lure, and he began catching salmon right and left. While the wife filmed, the younger son waded closer to see if he could get in on the action.

Soon Dad caught another fish, and the boy's frustration mounted as he crept closer to his father's fishing spot. By the time the fourth salmon was hooked the youngster was nearly in the old man's hip pocket, but still caught nothing.

Finally, Dad hooked his fifth fish, and the video records the boy's comment, "#$%@ *$#%#, I'M GETTING TIRED OF THAT!"

How To Plant A Chicken

I don't know who to believe: Hog producers who say their product should be the choice for healthy eating, dairy farmers claiming "milk does a body good," or bunny farmers suggesting rabbit meat will put a little more hop in your life.

I tend to believe them all. I like meats and dairy products and have a deep suspicion that all of them are good for us, if we eat them with common sense.

The part that throws me is when one group of meat producers claims their product has particular health benefits not possessed by other meats. The newspaper is full of that sort of thing.

Just recently I read about folks who are raising "hormone-free" rabbits. There's one for the books. If anything has hormones it's a rabbit!

I have reached the age where hormones don't scare me anymore; but if they did, I would stay away from rabbits.

The same week I read that water buffalo meat has 50% less cholesterol than beef and is cheaper to produce. I'd like to see the economic calculations on that one — as well as the research behind those cholesterol figures.

Then I saw a magazine article about European fallow deer. The article said meat from these deer contains no cholesterol. A wildlife column in a newspaper that same day showed deer meat having slightly more cholesterol than roast beef.

Fallow deer might be different, or either article could be wrong. Let's reserve judgment on that one.

Finally, to top it all off, I read that researchers at the University of Idaho are transplanting protein genes from chicken eggs into potatoes to create certain types of disease resistance in potato plants. What does that do to a vegetarian diet?

The idea of crossing chickens with potatoes reminds me of the fellow that wrote his local county extension office a few years ago. He wrote:

"I wanted to raise some chickens this spring, but am having problems getting them to grow. I planted the first shipment of chicks about four inches deep, with the rows two feet apart. None of them came up.

"A neighbor suggested I planted them too deep; so I put the next batch just under the surface with their heads above ground. These lived a few days, but grew poorly and finally died. I don't use commercial fertilizers or pesticides, so I know the ground hasn't been poisoned.

"What am I doing wrong?"

This was more than the county agent could handle; so he sent the letter to the university. After a few weeks a computer print-out arrived stating:

"Due to budget constraints we have not filled the agronomist position. Some people here think your area is too cold for raising chickens. If you wish to continue trying, be sure to get certified seed and have your soil tested."

Too Much Education

The hardest thing about spring is determining when to plant the garden. The second-hardest thing for many of us is getting the garden plot tilled or plowed.

For some reason it's even harder for farmers (or farm wives) to get their garden tilled than it is for suburbanites. This is because suburbanites have rototillers, while the farm wife has to wait for the old man to take down the fence so he can get that big old John Deere into the garden.

If you hang around farm stores this time of year, you will hear the familiar refrain, "I can't understand why a man can plow 500 acres to plant corn but he can't take 10 minutes to plow my garden." Most will say it's worth the wait though.

I'm sure rototillers prepare soil at least as well as a plow does, but there's something about the way a plow slices and rolls the soil that makes it more aesthetic for me. The old guys who did it with horses would probably say the old moldboard was even better with a big Percheron up front.

With today's huge machinery, plowing the garden ranks

right up there with shearing sheep for anticipation and excitement. The bigger the tractor and wider the plow, the more exciting it is. There's something about watching a guy with a new International and a 10-bottom plow pull into a garden that lends fervor to the whole thing.

I will never forget the first garden I planted — in the days when I was young and energetic and not real smart. I was just out of college and didn't have a tractor, so I decided to dig the garden with a spade.

We had about 40-by-80 feet of garden space, but planned on planting only half of it. I had turned a few shovels of soil when our neighbor came by, driving his John Deere and pulling a six-bottom plow. "We could take that fence down and I'd plow that patch up for you. It would save you a lot of digging," he said.

"Oh, no, I need the exercise. It won't take me long to dig it up," I told him.

I looked at his big tractor and thought, "He couldn't even turn that around in this garden. I'll have this soil dug up in no time."

When I was still digging a couple of days later, I began to wonder what sort of flaw in my upbringing had caused me to turn down the neighbor's offer. Why would a half-way intelligent person decide to turn several hundred square feet of soil with a spade rather than let the neighbor plow it up?

I was never valedictorian of my class or anything like that, but I did pass all the subjects.

Then, it dawned on me that my college training caused me to do it. I had been off to the university for four years, and it was so long since I had done any work that I had completely forgotten what it was like.

The Old Ones Were Funny

It's hard to overstate the effect of television on our society. A few weeks ago I listened to a political journalist describe the changes in national political conventions to accommodate television. This journalist covered presidential conventions for many years and has watched them adapt to the media.

This man says national conventions have reached the point where anyone who raises an issue is likely to be thrown out for insubordination. The main purpose for caucuses is to instruct state delegates on how to wave their signs and when to smile at the camera.

He also related a story about an elementary school teacher who won an award for his innovative teaching methods. The teacher discovered the best way to teach youngsters to read is to make a video tape of the text and then play it back on a TV screen.

He explained that today's children are so attuned to watching television they will watch almost anything if it comes through the tube. Opening a book is hard for them.

The teacher also commented he has considered dressing himself as a television for making class presentations, but he's afraid the little rascals will run up and try to change the channel.

All of this reminded me of my childhood during the early days of television. Readers may be surprised to learn I was hardly more than a toddler when television first became popular.

Before my family had a TV, we would walk to the neighbors about once a week to watch "Friday Night Wrestling" or "Midwestern Hayride." Of course cars were in common use by this time, but we usually walked.

Television was far more educational in those days. Midwestern Hayride for example featured people like Kenny Roberts, "the singing cowboy." Roberts could sing, leap into the air, chew gum, and play a guitar, all at the same time.

Perhaps Kenny's greatest talent was his ability to jump four feet in the air while strumming his guitar, without missing a note on the way up or down. He could wiggle his ears and wave his cowboy hat up and down, using nothing more than the muscles in his head.

We watched educational puppets like Kukla, Fran, and Ollie; and I'll always remember the old puppet who played the piano while keeping a lighted cigarette stuck to his lower lip. Now, there was a role-model for you.

This puppet was called Snarkey Parker (or something like that), and he had a horse than would come out and dance around on the stage or the piano, or whatever got in his way. All I can remember about the horse is that he ate some sticks of dynamite, thinking they were candy canes. He had old Snarkey worried for a while.

My kids wouldn't believe my stories about Snarkey Parker until we found him in a Smithsonian magazine this week. He was shown talking to Walter Cronkite in a 1950's news broadcast.

The kids still aren't sure about the singing cowboy and his hat-wiggling routine; but that's O.K. I never was real sure about him, either.

Sasquatch In A Sleeping Bag

It was the day before elk season, and I was standing in the hardware store listening to some old guys talk about their last minute purchases. "Do we need another game bag? Do you suppose this is enough cartridges?"

I got to thinking about my equipment. Which items do I really need, and which can I do without?

The answer was easy: the only thing I won't go anywhere without is "old Irey." Irey and I have been through thick and thin. We've seen enough thick smoke and thin pancakes to bring tears to the eyes of the toughest sheepherder.

Irey is my stove; and while I may forget anything from shirts to syrup, I won't go anyplace without my stove. Irey was made in Spokane, Washington and called the "Firey Irey" in its heyday. I bought the stove when I lived in Ohio and then spent several years learning how hard it is to outfit a sheepherder stove in a state that doesn't have sheepherders.

The first problem was the stove ring for my tent. These are supposed to be available at hardware stores or from any local outfitter.

We didn't have outfitters in Ohio as far as I could tell, and I soon learned that a person who would put a wood-burning stove in a tent is viewed with suspicion in hardware stores. I finally found a place in Columbus that sells asbestos cloth and persuaded my wife to sew a piece into the side of my tent.

Now, I was ready. My cousin, Dean, and I were going grouse hunting down near Lake Alma. There we would set up camp just like the guys in the outdoor magazines.

Anyone who is considering going camping with a man who has a new stove should talk with Dean first.

It wasn't so bad at first -just a little smoke coming out around the joints and through the vent on the door. As long as we stayed down near the floor of the tent, we could still breathe.

But then about midnight the wind came up, or the fire died a little, and Irey began to smoke in earnest. We pulled our sleeping bags over our heads and that helped. We still had smoke, but the down bags filtered out most of the tar and nicotine.

Finally, Cousin Dean commented, "Augh! Achh! *%^&@$ Smoke!," as he leaped to his feet and bounded through the tent door. (I would have opened the door for him if he hadn't been in such a hurry.)

It's a good thing the campground was deserted that time of year. A Sasquatch in a sleeping bag would have made good reading in the papers. Cousin Dean made several laps around the tent and came to rest on a picnic table, before he even looked for the zipper on his bag.

You can't blame Dean, really. He didn't plan to make a big scene. He just had a low tolerance for smoke.

I later cut a few inches off Irey's pipe and improved the chimney's exit-angle through the tent. After a few other minor adjustments, Irey and I became the best of friends and have enjoyed many a trip together.

Dean and I are still friends, too; but I was surely glad to see him settle down and get out of that sleeping bag.

Killed By Statistics

The President's recent visit to Iowa farms reminds me of the importance of personal contact when formulating government policy. Some folks may think the President was just politicking, but I like to see government officials sit down and talk with farm families. They learn so much more than they would from those gosh-awful statistics we keep seeing in print.

I remember politicians a few years back bragging that gross farm income was at an all time high. Anyone who talks with farmers soon learns how little gross farm income has to do with profit.

We have been badly misled by statistics. It's like the fellow with his feet in the oven and his head in the freezer: On the average he felt just fine.

The basic problem with statistics was impressed upon me a few years back when my sheep died. It was only one sheep, but the experience had a lasting effect on me.

It was early spring, and we were out of hay. I had plenty of hay in the fall for an average winter. Unfortunately no one has ever seen an average winter in this part of the country.

So I had to find something to feed the sheep, and all I had for pasture was a small patch of alfalfa with some early spring growth. That's when I started figuring, "If I turn the sheep out on that alfalfa they might die from bloat (a common ailment for ruminant animals eating young alfalfa). On the other hand, if I don't turn them out, they're gonna starve."

I had done some reading about bloat and alfalfa, and I knew this condition is unpredictable. Some animals inflate more easily than others, and even the inflatables often survive.

I also knew my sheep. They would rather die than see me get by with something.

This is where the statistics started going through my head. I had only three ewes. If one of them died that would be 33 percent of the flock.

A person who owns 300 sheep might lose 10 head in a really bad incidence of bloat; but that's only 3 percent of the flock. Nobody loses 33 percent from bloat. So I turned them out, and one old ewe died the first day.

The question is, "What killed her?" Was it the alfalfa? Did she die of bloat? That ewe was older than the others. Maybe it was just her time to go.

I will admit the symptoms of bloat were all there: Dead sheep, upside down, alfalfa all around. I'm sure a veterinarian would say she died from bloat of the frothy sort. In kindness, he might say the alfalfa did it.

That's the easy way out, though. You know as well as I do, I killed that old ewe. I did it with my statistics.

Hello, Dick Tracy

It's getting so a person has to have a CB radio or cellular phone to operate a farm or outdoor business. The advances in two-way communication have given every farm or business manager the opportunity to communicate with employees wherever they may be.

Being able to talk with employees in the field may seem like a great idea at first, but we should also recognize the problems this can create. We might remember that too much conversation isn't always a good thing.

Over lunch a few months back I listened to one farmer trying to convince another he needed a cellular phone in his truck. The first question asked by the second gentleman was, "Can everyone hear what I say?"

This may seem a trivial question unless you have listened to a radio scanner and heard what goes on out in the country. It can be real embarrassing.

The most awkward conversations are those directed back to the wife at base. "This is 8510 calling base, come-in base; 8510 to base, come-in base. Come-in base. Why isn't that woman ever home?"

"Ahh, drop dead! I'm washing my hair."

A more typical radio conversation goes like this: "Hello Bob, this is Warren. Ah'm all done moving the pipe. What should Ah' do now?"

"What is your location, Warren? Over."

"Ah'm in the truck. Over."

"I mean where's the truck, Warren? What field are you in? Over."

"Ah'm not in the field. Ah'm on a road next to a big ditch. There's another road on the other side; Ah' could be over there if Ah' drove over the ditch. Over."

"Don't drive over the ditch, Warren! What kind of field is across the ditch? Over."

"It's a pretty big one. Over."

"Can you tell me what's in the field, Warren? Over."

"Wul, I can see a tractor and a couple of trucks; but they're more on the edge. Ah' don't know if they's in the field or not. Over."

"No, Ah' mean what crop is in the field. Is it short and green or is it kinda tall and yeller colored? Darn it, Warren — now you've got me talking like that!"

"Ah'd say it's kinda tall and green, but not too tall. It's not exactly short, either. Considering it's a corn field, Ah'd say it's about right. Over."

"Do you have the pipe on the truck, Warren? Over"

"Ah' got some pipe on the truck, and Ah' put some next to that field you told me about. Over."

"Warren, do you know where the shop is? Over."

"Yeah. Ah' know where that is. Over."

"Good. You drive the truck over there and wait. I'll come down and talk with you."

One Man's Cross

I wrote a column a few years ago in which I mentioned a man dragging a cross with a wheel on it and walking along the side of the road. A few weeks later I received a letter from a lady in Virginia explaining that the man with the cross was Kevin Kinchen, a Texas evangelist, on a mission he calls A-Cross America.

The letter writer said Mr. Kinchen was written up in the January 1988 edition of National Geographic. A newspaper editor in California told my wife he saw this man on television. He said the fellow has a groove in his shoulder from dragging the cross around the country for more than 14 years.

It turns out I was writing about a famous person and didn't even know it. Here's a man who walks thousands of miles each year, converting people to Christianity, and I nearly run him down with my Subaru.

We have to admire the dedication of a man who would carry a cross until it made a groove in his shoulder. The only person I ever knew with that kind of determination was my agricultural economics professor, Dr. Baker.

Dr. Baker devoted a lifetime to studying the principles of economics and then trying to infuse them into farm boys with few principles of their own. Professor Baker's dedication is best illustrated by a farm survey he completed in northern Ohio many years ago.

Dr. Baker's study was completed spring semester, when farmers were in the midst of corn planting. Anyone who talks to farmers at planting time will tell you it's worse than converting heathens to Christianity.

A farmer told me one July day, "Sure, I can talk with you. There's only two times I can't stop to talk: Planting time, and harvest. Those two times of year, I'll run right over you."

Dr. Baker knew it was planting time, but he was working on a deadline. So he started down the road talking to farmers in the field.

He would see a tractor working and then walk out to ask the farmer some questions on his economic survey. Nobody ran over him, but he could tell they would have liked to.

Dr. Baker said the farmers would always stop to see what he wanted. Then after a few questions, they would start reaching for the throttle.

Readers might remember the early '60's was the era of the Johnny Popper: The John Deere A's and B's, later replaced by the Model 60 and Model 70. These old John Deeres had only two cylinders and produced a unique "kerpow — pow — pow" sound when idling. When you revved them up the Johnny Poppers would up the cadence to Pow! Pow! Pow! Pow!

Dr. Baker would get in a couple of questions during the idling pow — pow — pow's. Then the farmer leaned on the throttle, and Professor Baker shouted the rest of the survey to the tune of Pow! Pow! Pow! Pow! It was a nasty job.

I don't know what conclusions can be drawn from a survey conducted under those conditions; but it tells us something about the relationship between farmers and agricultural economists. I've noticed over the years that a farmer will do almost anything to keep from listening to an economist.

Spring Forward and Fall Flat

Fall is my favorite time of year. I enjoy autumn weather and the crisp fall mornings. Most of all I like fall because it's the time we get to set our clocks back to the correct time.

Daylight savings time may be a boon to the factory worker, but for me it's just six months of confusion. Each spring I have to ask my wife, "O.K. now, which way do we set the clock, forward or backward?"

"It's the same every year," she says. "Just remember, 'spring forward and fall back'."

I remind her that little jingle doesn't apply to people my age. I'm more likely to fall forward, and I don't spring anywhere.

But I set the clock forward for the summer because everyone else does; and it's pretty inconvenient to maintain your own personal time zone all summer long.

A farmer told me last summer, "You should do a column on daylight savings time. I think it's the craziest thing for the whole country to set the clocks up so people can go to work an hour earlier."

I can see his point. Farmers have always gone to work with the sun and quit when they had to. Setting the clock up an hour doesn't make a person any more industrious.

I didn't tell my farmer friend about the time I read my watch upside down and left my motel room at 1:30 A.M. to attend a meeting.

Despite only a couple hours of sleep, I was fresh as a daisy when I arrived at the motel restaurant. The place seemed strangely abandoned, and it was pitch dark outside.

I wasted no time getting back to my room and getting in bed, once I realized what had happened. It's embarrassing to get all dressed up and have no place to go.

Daylight savings time reminds me of the old joke everyone would spring on his fraternity brothers when we were in college. We would wait until the entire house had gone to bed and old Freddy was sound asleep. Then we would set his alarm clock forward an hour or two.

The other clocks had to be changed, too: his watch, the clock on the desk, and the one in the dining room.

Then, Fred gets up and heads off for class at 6:30 A.M. instead of 7:30. So here he is walking across campus wondering why there's no one else going to class. (Must be a big skip day.)

"The sun is a little late, too," he surmises. "It should be more light than this at 7:30 in the morning."

Then, it dawns on him: The clocks! Those slithering, sniveling roommates of his changed the clocks.

But it's too late. We've ruined his day. A good joke, huh?

It's the same trick Congress played on the country when daylight savings was instituted in the '60's. But we didn't get mad like old Freddy did.

We just ask feebly, "O.K., which way do we set the clocks, backward or forward?"

The Lap of Luxury

You just can't tell the rich from the poor anymore. Those things we used to think were luxuries have become standard equipment.

I read recently of a new project for low-income housing, where a county bought an old motel and is renting it out to those who can't afford other housing. Social service agencies are trying to help low-income residents by asking for donations of things like food, clothing, and microwave ovens.

While microwave ovens may be the most economical alternative for folks who don't have a kitchen range, I just can't get used to them as standard household equipment. I have always thought of them as a luxury.

I considered microwaves a luxury because we never had one — not until recently at least. My wife has always said she doesn't need a microwave and that's good enough for me. You won't find me spoiling a good woman with unnecessary frills.

But my mother-in-law couldn't stand her daughter being without conveniences, so she bought us a microwave. Actually, she bought it for my daughter who is in college; but we had the use of it for awhile.

Boy, talk about convenience! We soon got to the point where we couldn't get a meal together without the microwave.

The microwave thawed bread, heated up frozen leftovers, and defrosted meat.

And fast! You can take a leftover out of the freezer, zap it a minute or two in the microwave, and you've got a hot meal almost as good as the first time you ate it.

There's nothing like it for thawing things out. No need to worry about getting meat out of the freezer for dinner. When dinner time comes around, you just pull out a package and put it in the microwave. It's thawed in a few minutes.

But then my daughter went back to college and took the microwave with her — and we went into shock for a few days.

Now, when we want meat for dinner, we have to take it out of the freezer in the morning. If the hot-dog buns are frozen, we have to thaw them for a few minutes or put them in the electric range.

And leftovers — we don't eat many leftovers now that the microwave is gone. Now we cook the amount we want to eat, instead of making a huge batch and then zapping it for quick meals.

Once we got used to all that convenience it was real hard to go back to the old way of doing things. My wife commented one night at dinner, "We should have taken these rolls out of the freezer earlier. Too bad we don't still have the microwave."

"Well, I guess we can't have everything," I offered.

"Yeah," my son agreed, "We wouldn't need a microwave if we didn't have the freezer."

A Hard Winter

There's something about winter that puts people in a bad mood. Psychologists say the shortened day-length affects some segment of the brain or nervous system and causes people to feel depressed.

A newspaper publisher told me years ago, "We always get more complaints in January and February. Everyone's in a bad mood. People will get mad about things that wouldn't bother them any other time of year."

I try to remember this when writing winter columns. Not that I'm worried about complaints per se, but to be aware of my own moods. I learned years ago there's a thin line between being humorous or just a pain in the neck.

So I try to lighten up in the winter and get as much daylight as I can to keep my brain from congealing. That's why people go to Hawaii in the winter — so they can soak up the sunlight. These folks get lots of sun, spend all of their money, and return home with nothing left to worry about.

Psychologists say some winters are worse than others for

causing depression. Winters that are extremely cold, cloudy, or rainy are the worst. That's why long-range weather forecasting is so important.

If a person knew how bad the winter was going to be, he could head for Hawaii early and protect himself from the oncoming depression.

A scientific breakthrough in long-range forecasting was recently reported by Bill Felker, of Yellow Springs, Ohio. As author of "Poor Will's Almanack," Bill offered his readers $5 for the best techniques on predicting winter weather.

His top story so far is from Verden Smith of Findlay, Ohio. Mr. Smith says the best way to predict winter weather is by measuring tree bark.

"The simple way to do this is with a 16-ounce hammer and a kerosene lantern. (A flashlight will work, but it spoils the effect)," Smith states.

"At midnight on the dark of the moon closest to the middle of December, go outside with just your night clothes on and find a beech tree. If you can't find a beech — then a maple or oak will usually work just as well.

"Put your ear against the north side of the tree and give it a 'pound' halfway between your ear and the ground.

"If you hear a light 'arf' you have a thin bark, and a mild winter is in store. If you hear a reverberating 'Woof-woof' then you have a heavy bark. And if you haven't figured out it's a cold winter, you had better hurry inside before you freeze or the neighbors have you committed."

I sent Mr. Smith $5 for his bark story; and request that others who find similar use for this tale should send him something, also. He helped us get through the winter, and it's only fair that we do the same for him.

The Middle Class

Well, it's official now. We're going to have a presidential campaign after all. There was talk last fall that the Democrats were going to just give up, but now they're all packed-up and headed for New Hampshire.

You can always tell there's going to be an election when people start going to New Hampshire. Folks used to go up there for the maple syrup, but now somebody yells, "The sap is running!" and most anything can happen.

The big issue in this campaign is the middle class. Besides doing all they can for New Hampshire, each of the candidates wants to help the middle class.

They want to give us something so we won't feel bad about sending all that tax money to Washington, D.C. Nobody seems to understand that giving us stuff we didn't ask for is what makes the middle class so furious.

The tough part for the campaign strategists is deciding who is middle class. Middle class is like middle age: Ninety percent of the population thinks they qualify.

A news report says one campaign strategist thinks the middle class voter is a married suburbanite with $35,000 income, less than 45 years old, with a child or two, and a spouse who works also. Another says the typical middle class voter is 32 years old, works in a suburban office building, and has two kids in day care.

A more explicit definition of middle class is the 60 percent of Americans who have an income of $19,000 to $78,000 for a family of four. Regardless of definition, I've always identified with the middle class.

When I was a kid our school had about 80 students in each grade, and the principal divided us into three classes. The really smart kids were in one class, the dumb ones in another, and the rest of us were the middle class.

Our teachers treated the middle class the same way the politicians do. There was so much trouble with the dumb class, and so much potential in the smart class, that the middle class got the short end of everything.

This caused a lot of hard feelings and most of us haven't forgotten. Our class may not be smart, but we're long on memory.

If the campaign strategists knew what the middle class really wants, they would forget about income levels and whether the kids are in day care. They would cool the national health care rhetoric and suspend efforts to protect us from Japanese cars.

If the candidates honestly wanted to know, the middle class would say, "We'll send you to the White House on two conditions: First you have to stay out of New Hampshire for the next four years; and second, you must promise that you will never, ever, try to help us again!"

It's The Thought That Counts

"You need to buy your mother a gift," my wife said. "If you wait until the last minute you won't find anything she can use."

"We'll just send her some money. That way she can buy what she wants, and everyone will be happy," I suggested.

I don't know how it works for other men, but gift shopping is not one of my big things. It's only within the last few months that I would even venture into gift shops, and that has been to learn more about the book market.

It's a whole new world, I'll tell you — a woman's world where candle sticks and fluffy sheep jump out and say, "Buy me! You haven't bought anything all day."

What's worse, nearly all of these shops are operated by people with a thinly disguised passion for gifts. They stock their shop by attending huge gift shows where millions of items are displayed for sale. I'll tell you what, having these folks attend a gift show is just like sending a fox after the eggs.

My first experience with gift buying was many years ago when I was in high school. It was Mother's Day, and I was getting desperate. Some folks would have been desperate before this, but I was never one to get too far ahead with my shopping.

My mother isn't big on gifts, either. She always says, "It's the thought that counts." But a person needs some evidence of a thought, and our town had only one store that was open on Sundays.

Hill's Drug Store was quite a bit smaller than Macy's, with one counter in front, shelves down the walls, and some racks of clothing in the aisles. One shelf was full of alarm clocks and another harbored a big herd of stuffed animals.

I figured Mother had outgrown stuffed animals, and she already had an alarm clock. At least something was causing her to wake up and yell into my room each morning.

Then I noticed this thing that was hanging over the cash register. It looked a lot like a bird cage, but there was a plant in the center, which on closer inspection proved to be plastic.

Now, what would a person do with a plastic plant in a bird cage? I put it out of my mind while I explored the rest of the store, but finally I came back to the caged plant and bought it.

Mother said it was just what she needed, and she hung it right out on the porch where everyone could see it and bang their head on it if they wanted to. She said the plastic plant was real pretty and it surely was easy to take care of.

I've often thought back on that particular gift and wondered if my mother really liked it as much as she claimed. Some people would probably think a plant in a cage was about the silliest purchase a young man could come up with.

But now that I've been through a few gift shops and seen how those stores have to operate, I don't feel bad at all about buying that little monstrosity. The way I see it, the store bought it first; and if it weren't for guys like me they probably would still have it.

Demise Of The Dinosaurs

What could we talk about if it weren't for the weather and the dinosaurs? Just this week I read scientists now believe the dinosaurs helped create their own weather, thereby condemning themselves to extinction.

It seems an Indiana University geochemist found some fossilized dinosaur dung containing chemical signs of bacteria. This led to speculation that dinosaurs digested their food by fermentation, thereby producing methane gas.

If you've read about studies to determine amounts of methane produced by cows and the effects on global warming, you know the rest of the story. "What if dinosaurs produced so much gas they caused global warming and finally succumbed to heat exhaustion?" these scientists ask.

Beats the heck out of me. I thought they froze to death!

I can't speak for others but I've reached the point where I read the phrase "scientists now believe" and wonder what sort of nonsense is coming next. If scientists really believe the things we read in the newspaper, they aren't nearly as smart as we have been giving them credit for.

Dinosaurs have instigated some of the strangest scientific theories. First there was the asteroid theory. This thesis suggests the dinosaurs were standing around minding their own business when a charge of asteroids hit them like bowling balls from a giant scattergun.

The idea was first credited to a pair of quail hunters who stayed up too late loading shotshells; but now scientists are claiming it for their own.

Anyone who believes that one might consider the ice cube theory. This proposes that dinosaurs became so overpopulated they began scheduling cocktail hours each evening, so they could talk about the neighbors.

To obtain ice for their drinks, the beasts would break up two or three glaciers every day. The ravenous lizards finally destroyed both polar ice-caps, and then killed each other fighting over the olives.

Last but not least is the rainforest theory. This idea suggests certain dinosaurs were quite concerned about their environment.

These particular lizards told each other rainforests were being destroyed by plant-eating monsters (other dinosaurs). At the current rate of consumption these forests would be gone within a few hundred years and all of the dinosaurs would be extinct.

These dinosaurs collected money, held bake-sales, and threatened fast food restaurants until the rainforest was declared a wilderness area — thereby closing it to all activities except reading. This worked fine until the lizards who lived in the rainforest moved out into the surrounding countryside.

Displaced rainforest dinosaurs took most of the jobs, ate much of the remaining food, and started showing up at cocktail parties. One can imagine what happened next.

Those who can't imagine might wish to refer back to the ice cube theory.

Other Books by Roger Pond

IT'S HARD TO LOOK COOL WHEN YOUR CAR'S FULL
OF SHEEP   Tales From The Back Forty
(Humor)

THE LIVESTOCK SHOWMAN'S HANDBOOK: A Guide to
Raising Animals for Junior Livestock Shows
(Informational)

ORDER FORM

Pine Forest Publishing
P.O. Box 289
Goldendale, WA 98620
Telephone (509) 773-4718

Please send the following books.

Number of
copies

_____ THINGS THAT GO "BAA!" IN THE NIGHT

_____ IT'S HARD TO LOOK COOL WHEN YOUR
CAR'S FULL OF SHEEP

Your Name _____

Address _____

City _____

State _____ Zip _____

Please enclose a check or money order to *Pine Forest Publishing*
for _____ copies, at $9.95 per book plus $1.50 postage and
shipping for the first book. (Add $.50 postage for each additional
book.)

Washington residents add 7% sales tax.